Hope You Enjoy

Best Wishes

Dennis
Wright

Honeybee Books

Published by Honeybee Books
Broadoak, Dorset
www.honeybeebooks.co.uk

ISBN: 978-1-910616-13-0

Black Country Boy

Dedicated to Denise, Andrew and Barbara,
for their love and faith in my poetry

PREFACE

This poim yow see, woz ritten by me
Yow myt find it rayley ard gooin.
I cum from a towen with an axsnt
An it's a fust thing fower me that I'm dooin.
Om a black cuntry kid wi thorts in me yed,
Thorts that yowv praps ad yesen.
Oive neva put pen to a perpa
On most loikly wo do it agen.
This fust that oim ritin is me wots invitin
Orl of yow lot wiv me down me rode.
Poims that read mower loik storiz
In rime most a time to be tode.
Summa med up, an sumonem aye,
Sumonems barmy, yowl say.
It's me tek on loife as oive seen it
Os events thru the yaeres cum my way.
Me poims aye rittn loik this un,
I doe spake like this wen I rite.
I believe wot yow reed shud be eezy,
On eezy shud lede to delight

So now I'll revert to plain speaking -
My poems, I hope you enjoy.
The place I reside, I live there with pride -
Deep down, I'm a Black Country boy.

Dennis Wright, Dec 2014

CONTENTS

A REASON TO DIET

I'm trying to slim, I want to look thin,
I'm fed up with my look in the mirror.
My shirts are too tight and never look right
And I desperately want to look slimmer.
The chocolate and cake of which I partake
(Along with the burgers and fries),
Are making my waist expand with great haste
And my trousers now cling to my thighs.

It's easy to see what has happened to me
When I look at the food that I choose,
Although they taste great, the result is the weight
That I really must now try to lose.
The iced buns and crisps, fried chicken and chips,
Cream teas and the full Sunday roast,
The sandwich of bacon and hot bubbling cheese
That's invitingly spread on my toast.

My snacks between meals becoming the norm
And eating while watching TV,
The sweet bag that lives in its place in my car,
The biscuits that dunk in my tea.
The holes in my belt that never were used
Increasingly come into play, my waist has increased;
It is time that I ceased and finally called it a day.

The journeys not far that I drive in my car
Are easy and quick I can see,
But better would be to take a brisk walk
Which would be far more healthy for me.
The space in my wardrobe gets smaller
As I add more clothes to the rail;
There's nothing wrong with the clothes that I have
But to fasten them up is to fail.

Top buttons they hurt when I try on a shirt,
And the waist of my jeans far too tight.
The charity shops will gain at my loss
As my weight seems to grow overnight.
So now is the time to call to a halt
The eating of foods full of fat,
And change to a slimming and more healthy diet -
There's an abundance of foods that do that.

So I've made up my mind such foods I will find;
The salads, the pasta and fruit -
A much trimmer me in my mirror I'll see
Of a weight loss I'm in hot pursuit.

A RECIPE FOR CHANGE

Although I'm retired and have gone seventy three,
A new skill to learn is there waiting for me.
No shortage of tutors to get me away,
Just try to avoid them on telly each day.

For a real tasty dish
You can learn to cook fish,
Rick Stein is the tops, so it's said.
Paul Hollywood's skill with oven and grill
Bakes a mean tasty crusty white bread.
Fun you can poke at that spiky haired bloke
Gary Rhodes seems a figure of fun,
But I fancy a bash at his bangers and mash
And he sure bakes a great currant bun.
Hugh Fearnley Whittingstall sounds rather posh,
Though his cooking is basic and real.
His *River Side Cottage* could teach me some class
Cooking venison, partridge, and veal.

Can't Cook And Won't Cook, Come Dine With Me,
Hell's kitchen and *Nigella Bites,*
Food and Drink, Delia, Jamie At Home
And *Master Chef* on for five nights.
The Great British Bake Off and *Saturday Kitchen,*
Heston's Fantastical Feasts,
Hairy Bikers on Wheels,
Jamie's Five Minute Meals,
Ainsley Harriet's Culinary Treats.

I've watched Gordon Ramsey but really don't know
If what I have learned has a bearing.
The F Word has been a big influence I think,
'Cos I am increasingly better at swearing.
Chinese cuisine is no problem, Ken Hom taught me all I should know.
For a meal to eat later I watch Nigel Slater,
Simple Suppers for folks on the go.
Paul Rankin, Nick Nairns, Worral Thompson,
Tony Tobin, Ross Burden, Brian Turner
Would each show the way at tea time each day
Ready Steady's the place for a learner.

So now I am ready, I've bought all their books,
DVDs I have watched by the score.
I've lashed out a fortune at Kitchens 4 U -
My cupboards won't take anymore!
Saucepans and grinders, blow torches and mixers,
Mandolin, steamer and funnels,
With my Bain Marie, blender and pineapple juicer,
My kitchen is full to the gunnels.
Bread maker, ricer, cucumber slicer,
A full set of knives in a block.
I've got a terrine, a brand new tagine
And a large stainless steel Chinese Wok.

My first meal completed - oh, what a success!
It's a meal of which I can boast.
I've cooked it myself with my TV tuition -
Three rounds of cheese upon toast!!

CURE FOR SNAILS

Where do all these snails come from?
Why gather here at night?
Does sunshine bother them all day
And keep them out of sight?
My decking is their meeting place
And every night they call.
I can't remember going out
And see no snails at all!
Some are little, some are big,
And some without a shell.
Some are vivid orange -
And I've got those as well.
When trod on they go squishy
And stain my wooden floor.
So now I gently pick them up
And sling them all next door!

GARLIC

Garlic is great, it adds taste to your plate
And onions a hot sandwich filler!
But don't use them at all if bed's your next call -
Believe me, you'll find them a killer!
Beetroot and cheese makes me weak at the knees
And hot dogs with mustard sublime.
But what with the garlic and red teeth as well,
It scuppers my plans every time!

THOUGHT FOR THE DAY

Whenever words are hard to find
For thoughts deep in your head,
Put pen to paper, relax your mind
And write it down instead.
It doesn't have to be in rhyme -
It need not be too long.
Just say the things you want to say
That will not leave your tongue.

Words of love will mean as much
To someone you hold dear
When written down on paper
Or whispered in their ear.
"I love you" are just three words -
Three words with wondrous powers.
Three words that we can use each day,
Three words that now are ours!

I'VE GOT A CUPBOARD FULL

I bought some leather polish
And a tin of *Pledge* as well,
And a can of room refresher
With a new fresh, floral smell.
I didn't really need it but the offer seemed so good
(Buy the three and one came free!)
And so, I thought, I would.

My household cleaners all reside
In a cupboard 'neath the sink -
I've got the cure for everything
Or, so I like to think.

Finish tablets, *Finish* salt, and *Finish* lemon smell,
Parazone, *Domestos* and *Harpic*'s there, as well.
Washing powder, softener, *Comfort* and *Lenor*
And a laminate wood protector
To clean my wooden floor.

Windowlene and *Brillo Pads*, *Oxy Plus* and *Dettol*
And a cure for lime scale in a box
For my iron and my kettle.
A mould protector for my tiles
And a tin of *Shake n' Vac*,
Brasso, *Silvo*, *Cillit Bang*,
And scourers by the pack.

Oven cleaner, *Baby Bio*, kitchen rolls and *Flash*
And a super-duper grease remover,
If my frying pan should splash.
A stainless steel protector keeps my taps and sink top bright,
And a pack of six white candles
Should I need them one dark night.

Mr Muscle sink unblocker
Keeps my plugholes clean.
Fairy Liquid in three shades;
One red, one blue, one green.
J Cloths, dusters, rubber gloves, dishcloths, and *Febreze*,
A pair of strap on kneeling pads
(But I've found no use for these).
Ant spray, fly spray, *Hoover* bags,
Air Wick, *Oust* and *Glade*,
Room refresher refills for most that's ever made.

All these things I've gathered
And some things are a must,
But most of them sit idle and simply gather dust.
There isn't room for another thing,
The space won't take no more.
These three new tins, if I put them in,
I won't shut the cupboard door.

So now I've had a re-think,
And starting from today,
I'll sort the things I really need,
And throw the rest away.
Will *Windolene* clean my shower screen?
Is *Daz* as good as *Bold*?
Will *Brasso* clean my silver
And *Flash* treat surface mould?

Does it really matter if my *Fairy*'s green or blue,
Domestos versus *Harpic* to swish around the loo?
Will *Cillit Bang* shift lime scale,
Will fly spray kill the ants?
Can *Brillo* pads clean stainless steel
As well as pots and pans?
If my room should need refreshing,
To leave a pleasant smell
Do I need a can of *Air Wick*, *Glade* and *Oust*, as well?

So now I've made my mind up,
These things I'll buy no more
Till I find a multi cleaner
And can close my cupboard door.

A CAT'S TALE

I wish for a mistress to give me a home,
A mistress, who's gentle and kind.
In matters of food, I'm really not fussed,
Just a couple of things on my mind.
Some hake and best steak will do for a start,
And topside of beef will be fine.
Occasional salmon and fresh double cream
All served at a regular time.

My sleeping arrangements are simple;
A cozy warm rug by the fire.
A nice little place that is draught-proof,
Where, at night, I can relax and retire.
In return, she will see how good it can be
To have someone to fuss and to feed.
Love and affection, I've got lots to give
And love and affection we need.

So, if you're not fussy and want a stray pussy,
I'm here for the taking and free,
Open your door and open your heart;
Your choice of a pussy is me!

THE SETTEE

It's all a bit quiet at the moment
A time to reflect on my life.
I'm here in this bedsit apartment
And part of a young couple's strife.

I'm not feeling too well,
(If you look, you can tell),
I'm looking a bit worse for wear.
No longer the bouncy young thing that I was;
To be honest, I really don't care.

I'll come back later to this part of my life,
But let me go back to its start.
I was once the top model in *Harrods*
And stole a young newly weds' heart.

Along with two chairs I was chosen to be
The choice of a suite and the largest of three.
Dressed in fine leather, Italian made,
Bought without thought of the price to be paid.

In a Kensington mansion I made my debut,
My feet ankle deep in an Axminster new.
The top of range furniture, both front and aft
Were protected from harm from the sun and the draught
By the lined velvet drapes hanging down to the floor,
And the close fitting frame of a heavy oak door.

The circle of friends put us all to good use
When after their meal they'd retire.
Tales from the golf course, the theatre and bank,
Drinks in hand by a roaring log fire.

Cleaned every day when the maid came our way,
Our cushions plumped up, one by one.
In pristine condition the three of us stayed,
Till fashion decreed we'd move on.

Our next port of call was a shock to us all -
A farmhouse in Wales, none the less.
Bought as a bargain on *eBay*
For a knock-down fee, at a guess.

Far from the bright lights of London
And the pampered life we had known,
We were thrust in a van and transported
To start life in our new second home.

The house was in need of attention,
The room was dowdy and small.
The floor was bare, just a small carpet square,
And the paper hung loose on the wall.

When bought as a bargain on *eBay*,
No thought for our size had been given,
And room for us all there was no chance at all,
Our purchase was pure low-cost driven.

To get through the door, I was rolled on my side,
My castors removed to make way.
I was pushed, squashed and tilted to enter the room,
At my leather, I looked on with dismay.

Scratches and scuffs on my arms and my back,
My cushions strewn over the floor.
My mahogany trim looked decidedly grim,
With green paint from the frame of the door.

The same fate awaited one armchair -
He made a forced entry like me.
We were down to a duo, no space for a third
And no clue as to where he could be.

It was clear our new owners were different -
Their lifestyle was so far removed
From the Kensington couple we'd served for two years
In the house that we all three approved.

This farmhouse was home for a family of four;
A father, two sons and a wife,
Struggling to keep their business afloat
That was fast nearing the ending of life.

No gin and tonics were held in their hands,
No talk of the theatre or bank.
All meals were eaten in here off a tray
As into our cushions, they sank.

Overalls smelling of diesel
Next to my skin every day,
Footprints of boots on the worn, wooden floor
And a smell of manure-sodden hay.

An old gate-leg table and two dining chairs,
A TV that was well past its prime.
A striking clock that was minus its glass
And long since had forgotten to chime.

These were our only companions,
Their condition was plain, I could see.
I knew it was only a matter of time
Such condition would soon come to me.

But fate took a hand, in less than a month
The farm and the house repossessed.
We both ended up in an auction,
Along with the clock and the rest.

Lot twenty three was my number to be -
'A three seater couch' - no reserve.
The other two chairs had been sold in two lots
A fate that they didn't deserve.

My number came up, the hammer came down,
My price was insultingly cheap.
My bidder was pleased with his bargain
Then my cushions piled up in a heap.

In an open-top truck I was loaded,
I was off on the road, once again.
A large sheet of canvas pulled over my head
To protect from the drizzling rain.

The dust and dirt from the farmyard
Removed from my tired-looking leather.
Some soft saddle soap and a rose fragrant spray
Worked wonders when both used together.

From the rear of a shop I was carried,
Down the high street and through the front door
Of a takeaway outlet of Chinese cuisine,
To my pride of place spot on the floor.

The counter was tall and, behind in the wall,
A fish tank quite large with a light.
One lonely goldfish swam forward and back
Endless times through the day and the night.

A huge yellow board with prices and choice
Boldly displayed over my head.
The flock-covered walls in Chinese design,
In a deep shade of velvety red.

Magazines and papers to read while you wait,
A TV tuned in, without sound.
All this would be a new venture for me
In this strangest of places I'd found.

The takeaway custom that came through the door
Would make themselves comfy on me.
A ten-minute stay and they'd be on their way,
And a seat for the next would be free.

All kinds of people came in off the street -
New acquaintances made every day.
Like musical chairs, I played out my part
As a turn on my seats came their way.

Sharp-suited businessmen, drivers of cabs,
Pensioners, builders and teachers,
Big Issue sellers, along with bank tellers
And occasional hungry lay preachers.

Firemen, policemen, lollipop ladies,
Revellers in from the pub,
Football followers and out-of-work actors;
All shoulders, with which I would rub.

Seven days a week I encountered them all;
Used and abused, sad to say,
My appearance became rather shabby,
It was clear time was near to make way.

Without ceremony or thanks for my use,
I was carried outside to a skip,
Destined to end my last journey quite soon
In a crusher at some council tip.

Perched on the top of unwanted junk,
I awaited the chains and the lift,
But destiny moves in mysterious ways,
And mine proved to be a strange gift.

A young woman and man looked me over
Then wrestled me down to the street.
Without more ado, I was pushed sixty yards,
My next home in a flat, I would meet.

This brings me back to the start of this tale,
My new life begins again here.
Oblivion awaited for me in that skip,
But a lifeline's been thrown and that's clear.

A bathroom and kitchen, a bedroom-cum-lounge,
An old chemist shop down below.
A love-struck young couple with plenty of zest,
Starting out on a budget that's low.

The room freshly papered, the paintwork redone,
Bright curtains look out to the street.
A make-believe coal fire plugged into the wall,
While a cat made the most from the heat.

My seating removed to transform me,
Hidden secrets revealed in my base;
Tell-tale reminders of where I have been,
My adventures are easy to trace.

Along with the fluff and the breadcrumbs,
The biro, the ring pulls and coins,
The takeaway menu, a bus pass and comb,
Lay a treasure of worth in my loins.

A brooch of pure gold, encrusted with stones -
Who knows what its value would be.
But finders are keepers in worn-out settees
And a gift to this couple from me.

A home machined cover stretched over my frame,
A match with the curtains, so bright.
With cushions zipped up in a tight-fitting case,
I am sure my new life will be right.

So, here I am now, looking modern and new
With pride, as I look round this room.
I have come a long way from *Harrods* that day
When I enchanted the bride and the groom!!

NO?

&

No	long sunny days
No	grass fires ablaze
No	blossoms of peach
No	kids on the beach
No	daylight at five
No	butterflies thrive
No	pollen to sneeze
No	warm barmy breeze
No	swallows on wing
No	cuckoo to sing
No	chorus at dawn
No	bikinis are worn
No	barbecue nights
No	ugly gnat bites
No	swimmers in sea
No	wasp and no bee
No	cornfield to see
No	leaf on a tree
No	wonder
No	vember !!!

THE END OF A BEAR AFFAIR

I'm a lifelong fan of *Rupert Bear*,
I think to some excess.
I've gained his ways from early days
In Beaverbrook's *Express*.

I find my conversation,
In a period of time,
Is quite absurd - for all that's heard
Are words that always rhyme.

I'll give to you a thing or two
To show you what I mean,
And reactions to my actions
In the shops where I have been.

"Good morning, Mr Milkman -
How are you today?
I'll have two pints of pasteurised
And tell you - if I may -
I'm waiting for the postman,
He's really rather late
And on your way back to your cart,
Please shut my garden gate."

My next door neighbour's not too well,
I'll go round to her door
And ask if I can carry home
Her shopping from the store.

"I need some ham, some fruit and jam,
And pills, to ease my tension,
And pop into the postal shop
And get my old age pension.
Your rhyming slang is catching -
It's really got to stop.
That yellow scarf looks daft on you -
Now clear off down the shop."

I think she's right about the rhyme,
And, yes, it's getting worse.
Now everyone I come upon
Is answering me in verse.

So, now I have decided
This habit has to stop,
But not before I tell them all
(When I go in their shop)
What I really think of them,
Polite, no more I'll be,
Although I might not want to hear
Just what they think of me

"Good morning, Mr Baker,
I'm cancelling my bread.
That loaf you sold me yesterday
Was stale and hard as lead.
Your choice of cakes - abysmal,
Your crisps are out-of date.
Have a nice day, I'm on my way,
I'm running rather late."

"Your custom here will not be missed
You never buy much bread.
Your ears are big, your jumper's tight
And a lousy shade of red."

"Hi there, Mr Grocer man,
I thought you'd like to know
I won't be shopping here no more,
I've somewhere else to go.
Your choice is small, your shelves too tall -
My minds made up and so,
I'll go to town upon the bus
And shop with Mr *Tesco*."

"I'm sorry that our service
For you has fallen flat,
But I'm glad to see the back of you,
I'm very sure of that.
You never, ever spend much -
Your rhyming is a pain.
I hope you miss your *Tesco* bus
And don't come here again."

"Hello there, Mr Butcher,
I think you ought to know
Your sausages are mostly bread,
And their pork content is low.
Your beef is tough and hard to chew,
Your bacon has no taste
And money spent within your shop
Is really quite a waste."

"I'm glad that you've decided
To shop for meat elsewhere.
Your stupid rhyming makes me mad -
Of your dress sense I despair,
With your checked, bright yellow trousers,
And your fake bright orange tan,
You make Dale Winton look quite pale -
It's about time you began
To ditch your scarf and jumper
And make your rhyming stop.
Find another butcher,
And clear off out my shop."

It's over now - I think I'm cured,
My *Rupert* days are over.
My scarf and shoes and yellow trews
And beloved red pullover
Are surplus to requirements -
They've all gone in the bin.
But, I fear this year a change is near
'Cause I've started reading *Tin Tin*!

THIS LITTLE PIGGY STAYED AT HOME

A family of ten with me in this pen,
There's plenty of food to be found.
There's heaters above to keep us all warm
And plenty of straw on the ground.
We haven't a Mom, for sadly she's gone -
Who our Dad is, we haven't a clue -
But I know why I'm here and my vision is clear
And I know just what I'm going to do.

At the moment it's fine, I was fifth in the line
And together, were weaned for a time.
But once we were able to fend for ourselves
Our life span went into decline.
Our purpose in life is just part of a plan
To rapidly grow to a size.
Then along with the others, our day will arrive
And together, we'll meet our demise.

In this warm, sheltered sty, we will stay for a while
'Till we all are a suitable weight.
Then, replaced by a litter of newly born pigs,
Who are destined to have the same fate.
Out in the meadow, surrounded by wire,
It stings to the touch and it's clear
We may be free to roam, but for now this is home,
And our growing to size will be here.

A galvanised pen (about five by ten),
Is our shelter and bed for the night.
We are not on our own and never alone,
There are hundreds all in the same plight.
The food is abundant, there's water to drink,
Fresh hay is in daily supply.
There's plenty of mud to make us feel good
And loads of clean straw for our sty.

All of our needs are looked after,
From vitamins through to the vet.
Our welfare is paramount to all concerned,
As bigger and bigger we get.
A ride in a lorry that drives through the gate -
It seems, is the ultimate prize.
But you cannot partake unless you can make
The obligatory weight and the size.

An uncomfortable ride, when packed tight inside,
But finances determine the load.
The journey is short - they all harbour the thought
That for them it's the end of the road.
By then it's too late, for the abattoir waits,
For those who were fatefully bred.
Their halcyon days are all over -
The food chain about to be fed.

So, here in this meadow, my life I'll prolong,
In my mind, I have nurtured a plan.
I'll eat what I need and say *no* to greed,
And stay slim as long as I can.
The weight bursting food that's on offer,
I'll leave for the others to eat.
I'll manage on grass and that lorry will pass;
Slim pigs are no good to make meat!

TIME FOR A CUPPA

Don't make my tea in a cup, love,
I know it's so easy to do.
But that's not for me, for I like my tea
Made in a teapot to brew.

A bag in a cup is no good, love,
When you whizz it around with a spoon.
It's always too strong if left in too long
And too weak, if discarded too soon.

The cup is too hot to handle,
The tea is scaldingly hot.
When the teabag's took out, I feel cheated;
In my cup, there's less tea than I'd got.

Don't make my tea in a cup, love -
Milk and sugar, I like to add first,
But the teabag soaks up all the sugar
And the milk seems to come off the worst.

Don't make my tea in a cup, love,
There's a problem we need to address;
A steaming hot bag - where to put it?
Anywhere looks a bit of a mess.

So, don't make my tea in a cup, love,
Just leave it to brew in the pot,
And let *Starbucks* see that their making of tea
They can keep, if they like it or not!

TRUE LOVE

I'd walk into fire,
Trudge through the deep mire!
Fight tigers with just my bare hands.
I'd sail stormy seas,
Grab a hedgehog with fleas,
And listen to lousy brass bands.

Deep oceans, I'd swim
And - just on a whim -
I'd climb up the Eiger on stilts.
I'd squeeze *Desperate Dan*
'Till that brute of a man
Gives up and his strength simply wilts.

I'd wrestle with snakes,
Drive *Grand Prix* without brakes,
And the North Pole, I'd trek 'till I'm blue!
Then, in my bare feet,
Hot coals I would treat
With contempt, on my way to see you!

And so, you can see, how things are with me,
My courage, you'll never find waning.
I'll see you this Sunday, come hell or high water,
Unless it should start *!?*!?*! raining!!

THE VAGRANT

The bedraggled figure slowly trudged,
The footprints left his mark.
The snow whirled round in circles,
The street was all but dark.

His hands thrust deep in pockets,
Head bowed and shoulders hunched,
The icy wind showed no respect,
And through his clothing, punched.

His bed roll in a duffle bag,
Its drawstring pulled up tight,
Would help deter the bitter cold
This snowy, winter's night.

His cardboard bed in the railway arch,
Where he slept the night away,
Was about a mile from the bench in town
Where he whiled his time by day.

His fingers ached from the biting cold,
But were clenched to hold on tight
To the coins dropped in the worn peaked cap,
By those with thought for his plight.

Foreboding buildings flanked the street,
No windows shed a light,
The derelict factory looked austere
In the yellow-tinted night.

The railings and the padlocked gate -
Bathed in the amber glow
Of the sparse street lamps - were covered now
With a coat of glistening snow.

The worn-out boots, now ankle-deep,
Let in the cold and damp.
He crossed the road towards his arch,
And halted 'neath a lamp.

His way was blocked some yards in front -
A car had left the road.
Two wheels straddled across the path
That led to his abode.

Between the glow of the red tail lights,
A figure hunched up tight
Tried, in vain, to free the car
From its snowdrift-grasping plight.

The engine roared, the wheels spun round,
The car rocked to and fro,
The polished ice would give no grip
To release it from the snow.

He reached the scene to offer help -
The figure turned around.
A well-dressed woman, clearly stressed,
Whose breathing was profound.

A broken shoe lay in the snow,
Its high heel at an angle.
Her coat, wet through from falling snow,
Her hair all in a tangle.

The engine ceased, the wheels stopped spinning,
The driver stepped outside.
Despair was etched upon his face -
Despair he couldn't hide.

A dinner suit, a frilly shirt and shoes of patent leather,
Not fit for purpose this cold night,
In winter's worst of weather.
The vagrant offered up his help,
His offer well received.
No question of just who he was,
No thought of him perceived.
The bed roll pack he opened up, the blanket he unrolled,
Then tucked one end beneath a wheel, while kneeling in the cold.
The driver started up the car, the wheel began to spin;
It took a grip of the tucked in end
And pulled the blanket in.

Standing in the drift of snow, the gear set in reverse,
The vagrant heaved to give assist with a lowly, uttered curse.
The bed roll blanket drawn beneath, the wheel spin gave a stutter,
The car retreated in its tracks and bounced down to the gutter.
His blanket had succeeded, but lay there in a heap,
Wet and torn, no further use, when laying down to sleep.

One shoe on and one shoe off, the woman took her seat.
The driver beckoned to him, as he stood there in the street.
"Forget that bed roll, climb inside," he opened up the door.
"I need to talk with you, my man, I've seen your face before."
The vagrant took his hat off, stamped the snow from off his feet,
Ran fingers through his tousled hair and slumped into his seat.
The interior light lit up the face of the driver of the car,
And memories came flooding back, of places from afar.

A new recruit in a fighting force, a soldier; young and raw,
The acrid smell of burning flesh, and a bitter Falklands War.
The face bereft of greasepaint, but still that ice-cool stare,
The cultured voice he recognised, with its commanding, stable air.
The dress suit and the bow tie, faded out of view.
In a combat suit and a green beret, he became the man he knew.
The exploding shell rang in his ears, and four reduced to two.
No commanding voice to take control, but he knew what he must do.

The armoured car had took the blast, the fire raged from below.
Two comrades paid the price of war and an injured, trapped CO.
The driver's door was open wide, he stumbled from his seat,
Ran round to the other side and in the searing heat,
Released his CO from the wreck and dragged him to the ground,
And strength to carry him from the wreck, improbably, he found.
The CO lay unconscious, his plight was plain to see,
The gaping wound was oozing life from ankle to the knee.
Around his thigh, his combat belt he placed and tightly wound,
Then called once more on inner strength to gain a higher ground.

Fatigue then claimed the upper hand, the two soldiers lying prone,
The armoured car burned fiercely, as he heard an engines drone.
The rotor noise rang in his ears, his eyes they wouldn't see,
The final thought as rescue came, "There's just big Jim and me!"

"What the hell are you about? What brought you to this low?
Where's the guy who had it all? Where's the guy I know?"
"Start this car and let's head home," the woman intervened.
Her hair now brushed back from her face,
Smudged make-up roughly cleaned.
"Discuss such things in comfort when you're both dried and fed,
Not in the confines of this car, but in the warmth instead."

The iron gates swung open, the house was all aglow,
Tyre tracks left behind them in the freshly fallen snow.
The front door opened for them, a young girl dressed in black,
A frilly apron round her waist, in a bow tied at the back.
With a welcome smile, she took their coats and hung them on a stand,
Then led the way along the hall, to a room both large and grand.
Fine furnishings and décor gave out expensive feeling,
A baby grand with lid upraised and an ornate painted ceiling.
Plush leather seating, velvet drapes, oil paintings on the wall,
The trappings of a wealthy house, this one room said it all.
The open fire was slumbering, but with a skilful poke
Burst into life with dancing flames, and then the vagrant spoke;

"It's twenty years since last we met, the date of my de-mob.
I went back home to Civvy Street, my family and a job.
Life was good for eighteen years, our boy had reached his teens,
Our rented house, we'd given up for the house of all our dreams.
To celebrate this milestone, this house to call our own,
We dined out at a swanky place, a mile from out of town.
We splashed out on the menu, we had the best they'd got -
Caviar, champagne and red wine - we had the bloody lot.
We stayed on late and partied, well into the night,
The three of us were overjoyed, and all was good and right.

"Driving home was not so good, my vision was impaired.
No road marks on the country lane, and through the glass, I stared.
Too much champagne, too much wine, I know it now to be.
The road bend missed, the lost control, and the unforgiving tree.
For two years I've re-lived it all, two years I've lived in hell.
My reckless driving cost the lives of my wife, and son, as well.
I lost my licence, lost my job, and spent six months inside.
No return to the rented house, it's now re-occupied.
Friends and foes forsake me, the drinking eases pain.
Eighteen years I had it all, and now gone down the drain."

In a wing-back chair, the CO sat, his wife, there by his side.
She listened to events throughout, and openly, she cried.
He stood and faced the vagrant, and in that cultured voice,
He sympathised with all he said, and offered him a choice.

"Continue on your downward path with guilt etched in your heart,
Or take this hand I offer you, and make a brand new start.
Employment's not a problem, for here on this estate
Are lots of jobs that you could do, at a healthy going rate.
There's a flat for your disposal, it's offered you rent free.
I owe you one - so now, come on - throw in your lot with me!"

Through clouded eyes, the vagrant stared at the CO's welcome face,
Gratitude and honesty - of disdain, there showed no trace.
The trust in him in battle, still smoldered in his smile,
And now the chance to change this life and go that extra mile.
To find the life he'd left behind, to get life back on track,
Look forward to a better time, instead of looking back.

He brushed a tear from off his cheek, his outstretched hand was steady;
To grasp the hand and seal the deal, his mindset now was ready...

RUG HEAD

You might think I am loony,
But I'm following Wayne Rooney
And cultivating growth upon my bonce.
I'm sick of being called all the terms that go with bald,
And I want it looking like I had it once.

My pension pot can't stand the withdrawal of thirty grand,
So a cut-price solution I have found.
I got it from a bargain store, it's used for growing plants,
And like everything they sell, it cost a pound.

I've used it for a fortnight, results are looking good -
There's a covering of growth instead of sheen.
The only trouble is the colour don't look right -
If there's one thing that don't suit me, that is green.

It's growing very quick and it's getting very thick,
And, in no time, will be covering my ears.
But, advice from Alan Titchmarsh has found, for me, the cure;
So, I'll trim it twice a month with garden shears.

SEEMED A GOOD IDEA AT THE TIME

A hot sunny spell, the forecast was good,
An outing was planned for the day.
We'd head for the seaside and soak up the sun,
And a picnic we'd have on the way.

The buckets and spades were safe in the boot,
The hamper was full to the brim.
A tank full of petrol, the kids in the back,
The Sat Nav - finely tuned in.

Our start was delayed when the keys were mislaid
And our six o'clock start went to seven -
In a bucket I found them on searching the boot
And the eyes of the wife looked to heaven.

The roads were quite quiet as we left the estate -
Our journey won't take very long,
But joining the motorway five miles ahead,
I could see straight away I was wrong.

Three lanes of traffic all going our way
And, to hazard a guess, looking round,
That the caravans, roof racks and trailers suggest
That the coast, for the most, they were bound.

Bumper-to-bumper, all lanes were the same,
Our progress was slow to a fault.
Ten miles an hour for mile after mile,
And sometimes were brought to a halt.

Why is it, when traffic starts moving
And your journey proceeds at a pace,
Just what was the cause of the hold-up
For there seems to be not a trace.

The kids were both getting restless,
The *I Spy* game a bit of a bore.
The fruit gums had long since been eaten,
And the wrappers were strewn on the floor.

The wife's legs were crossed, her eyes glued to the signs.
I knew the next thing I must do -
Find the next exit and make a bee line
To a place we could stop for the loo.

The hands on the clock had motored along -
The seaside was still far away.
A sign for the Cotswolds we followed,
And decided to there spend our day.

We stopped at a pub, made use of the loo,
And a place for our picnic we found
At a riverside spot with a tree for the shade
And our blanket, we spread on the ground.

The hamper we took from the boot of the car,
Its contents were all neatly packed;
Sandwiches, crisps, fizzy drinks and cream cakes -
There was nothing that this hamper lacked.

Throwaway plates and *Tupperware* boxes,
Plastic cups and a flask,
Ready-made salad all suitably washed -
All that a picnic could ask.

The plates all passed round to all sitting down,
Everyone soon tucking in.
But the lure of the salmon that wafted around
Would soon tempt a wasp to the tin.

With a high buzzing sound our guest flew around,
His choice was so varied to make.
He tasted the ham and the strawberry jam,
Then sampled the cream in the cake.

With a swipe of my hand before he could land
On a slice of pork pie on a plate -
His progress was brought to a shuddering halt
And his landing determined his fate.

In a beaker of *Coke* he'd attempt the breast stroke,
But his efforts were ended quite soon.
Unable to fly, he was squashed up the side
With the back of a white plastic spoon.

I felt rather smug, as I looked in the mug,
This threat to our picnic decreased,
But I didn't know the last dice he would throw
Was the threat that would make it increase.

The signal he'd sent before his demise
To his mates close at hand, soon would be
A reason to leave in a hurry
And an end to our afternoon tea.

In their striped yellow jackets they came in their droves,
Invited to be at his wake.
The bonus would be the remains of our tea -
The pork pie, the crisps and the cake.

We swatted and swiped as much as we could -
The kids took off down the field,
But, try as we may, they had come here to stay
And this feast, they just weren't going to yield.

We snatched up the blanket and shook it -
The containers were gathered together.
Then, to add to our woes, the sun disappeared
And signalled a change in the weather.

The dark clouds descended, hung low in the sky,
The wind took a turn for the worse -
Big spots of rain increasingly fell
And our tempers increasingly terse!

Soaked to the skin, the kids clambered in,
The lightning lit up the sky.
In no time at all, the field turned to mud
And our need of an exit was high.

The track we had followed had now disappeared,
The water spread over the field.
On nearing the gate where we entered,
The ground 'neath the wheels, it would yield.

Down to the axle, with wheels spinning round,
We both cursed the wasps and the rain.
Then the driveshaft gave way and the engine cut out
Due to the heave and the strain.

We waited an hour for help to arrive
In the form of the road rescue van.
No chance of repair, we were winched in the air,
By that nice polite *RAC* man.

Our travel back home less eventful
On the bench seat we sat looking back.
Our car followed behind, its wheels off the road,
Held up on a hydraulic jack.

We arrived back at home early evening,
Abandoned the car for the night -
The buckets and spades and the hamper
We would retrieve next day in the light.

Twelve hours before, as we locked the front door,
We had no idea this would be
A day when events would be etched in our life
Of a day trip down to the sea!

SPRING HAS SPRUNG

As daylight breaks through each morning
And birds begin to sing,
Each day grows longer - night recedes
And winter turns to spring.

The fallen leaves, no longer gold
Lie dead upon the ground.
New buds appear upon the trees
And shoots, from bulbs, abound.

The frosty mornings fewer now,
Replaced by morning mist.
Gardeners wait - anticipate
And review their needful list.

The greenhouse gets its springtime clean,
Its windows bear the sign.
Algae blocking out the light
Built up through wintertime.

Plant pots washed and sterilised,
Seed trays all made ready.
Bags of compost stacked inside
And heating turned on steady.

Early sowings can begin,
The pale sun gains more yellow.
Everywhere there's signs of spring
As weather gets more mellow.

Worm castes brushed from dormant lawns,
Mower blades are honed.
Cuttings set in gritted trays
And precious plants are cloned.

Grass begins its upward trend,
At first, just slow and steady.
Snowdrops fade and disappear
And daffodils get ready.

'Ne'er cast a clout till May be out',
Or so the old saying goes,
For winter can bite back sometimes,
So be prepared - who knows!

THE KEY

If your life seems to be at a standstill,
And the hours in the day seem long,
Think back through the years - the laughter, not tears -
Take steps to put right what is wrong.
An impossible task, to turn back the clock,
Keep memories deep in your heart.
Life's like a book, it's in chapters -
There's a new one for you now to start.
The places you've been, the sights that you've seen,
The friends and the people you've met,
You surely will find are etched in your mind
And you're moving on forward affect.

'Life must go on' and 'time, it will heal'
Mean nothing, when spoken to you.
But experience tells me both things you will find
In time, will turn out to be true.
The healing will never be perfect,
The life ahead, no-one can know,
But there's really no doubt you will never find out
Till your past life, you gently let go.
Ventures anew may seem alien to you,
But try them and, in a short while,
You will find that these ventures could be pastures new
And a reason to bring back your smile.

Do not lose touch with friends and relations;
Don't spend endless hours looking back.
Meeting new people and making new friends
Will help get your life back on track.

If you look, you will find there are groups of all kind
Who will extend a warm welcome to you;
Subjects and leisures you already know -
For a challenge, try something that's new.
The list is unending, the subjects diverse,
And membership be large or small,
But each has an asset beneficial to you,
An asset that's open to all.

In all groups you will find there are people
Like you, with a lot on their mind
And willing to share with genuine care
Their thoughts of a life left behind.
Thoughts of a future as yet the unknown
And problems you both now may face.
Talking it out is the right way to go
As your new life starts falling in place.
Poetry, music and walking; keep fit, slimming and dance,
Camera clubs, travel clubs, volunteer aid -
Your spare time will surely enhance.

If some of these things you feel aren't for you,
Or you're really not up to the task,
Make up your mind, then go out and find
A choice to suit you and just ask.
The key to them all is the friends you will make,
Hidden talents you may well expose.
Hours of enjoyment and pleasure you'll find,
And we all need plenty of those.
But friendship's the heart of the movement
And friendship is surely the key.
Glad tidings and troubles are much better shared,
And friendship don't cost - it's for free!

THE LATE SAINT VAL

Sound in mind, with heavy heart,
On a day, long since gone by,
Saint Valentine sent words of love,
For he was doomed to die!

A sonnet written on a card,
His lady love received.
And so it was, *Saint Valentine*'s
Was long ago conceived.

Alas for Val, too late it was,
Delivered to her door,
She never got the wretched card
'Till Val, he was no more!

For, in those Roman days of old,
I hope you understand,
The penny post had not begun,
All letters went by hand!

The lowly serf who did this job
Was found the night before
In drunken stupor, lying prone
Upon the ale house floor.

He rose at noon, his work to do,
His feet they felt like lead.
"These letters in my pouch can wait -
I'm going back to bed!"

Next day, he took Val's words of love,
The maiden read the note.
Now she knew just how Val felt,
And donned her hat and coat.

A day too late she reached the jail,
Her feelings to return.
Val was dead and thought that she,
His words of love did spurn.

So, to this day, we live this tale,
We send our words of love.
And as we do, just take a while
To read this tale above.

For - just like Val - and one day late,
I send these words so true,
This tale of love and passion
Is between just me and you!

So, let us keep it secret,
Don't spread the word around.
Saint Valentine's, on the 15th day
Each February, can be found.

WHY ME?

I don't know what it is with me, my face just seems to fit,
Whenever there's a need for help, it seems that mine is it.
I went to Monet's garden to see a touch of class,
They were short of staff and roped me in to help them cut the grass.
On a weekend trip to London, I went to *Harrod*'s store
Mingling with the posh and rich, I stood and held the door.
People thanked me kindly, as they sauntered through the shop,
It was half-past five when I loosed the thing, when trading had to stop.

A disaster at the theatre was soon to come my way,
Thirty quid gone wasted at a Harold Pinter play.
The bloke who sat down next to me was suddenly taken ill,
"Would someone help take him outside?"
"Of course," I said, "I will."
I helped him in a taxi, and sent him on his way,
Then tried to get back to my seat and sit and watch the play.
However, it had started, and the rules - they are a fact -
No-one enters 'till the play begins the second act.

I cleared the snow from off my path, one winter's day last year.
I did next door's (she's ninety four) and needed help, poor dear.
Then one-by-one, they all tagged on, as the cold got to my feet,
And before I hardly realised, I'd cleared the flippin' street.

At a football match played in the park, I stood and watched the action.
They asked me if I'd help them out - and 'yes' was my reaction.
But, silly me, I didn't see, as the players all stood back
I was introduced as the bloke to be; the official all in black.

On a night out at our local club, I'd gone to socialise.
The cabaret act came straight to me and looked me in the eyes.
"You're in my power," he softly said, his presence was amazing.
My knees went weak, I couldn't speak and my eyes soon started glazing.
His magic's known worldwide, it seems - I believe just what they say.
He put me in a trance that night, and I woke at noon next day.

The final straw was bonfire night helping build the fire,
Collecting wood from the neighbourhood, dressed in old attire.
Feeling tired I rested, on a bench upon the street,
My woolly scarf around my neck and my hat down by my feet.

I accept that I looked scruffy, but it nearly made me cry
When two pound ten went in my hat as 'penny for the guy'.
So, now when help is needed - I look the other way,
And leave the task to someone else to help to save the day.

Oh, Donkey

I wish that I could make things clear
And my language understood,
To make my feelings plain to see
Would make my life so good.

Free to do just what I like,
To eat and sleep at will,
Decide just when I want to walk,
Or relax and just stand still.

To feel the sun upon my back,
The rain and wind avoid,
The endless bedlam in my ears,
Just makes me paranoid.

Places new I would like to view,
New faces would be good.
Romance and love I'd like to try,
And if I could, I would.

Deciding when my day will start,
Deciding when it ends,
No repeated journeys every day
On a road that has no bends.

When to eat and when to drink,
I'd really like to be,
Things that I decide myself
At times that just suit me.

Big fat ladies, screaming kids,
Macho yobs galore,
Use my body at their will
Through summer 'till the fall.

To what's-his-name that leads me on,
I'm just a cash machine
To fund a life of luxury
And fulfil his every dream.

He doesn't care just how I feel,
He'd never dream to ask.
Each day's the same, I end up here
To do the same old task.

How much longer? I don't know,
But a certain fact is that -
When my time has come
He'll replace me quick,
And I'm very sure of that.

Just who am I to sit and cry
For a life that's out of reach,
Just a stupid donkey
On another seaside beach!

MORNING

The kettle whistled endlessly, the milk began to rise,
From the bedroom door, the boy emerged, still rubbing at his eyes.
"If you're not washed and down here soon," his harassed mother said,
"At seven o'clock tonight, my lad, I'll pack you off to bed!"

"Every morning's just the same, when it's time to go to school,
You lie in bed then dally round while I - just like a fool -
Clean your shoes, and make your tea, your breakfast then prepare -
And tell our Jean to shake a leg while you are still up there!"

A horrid smell came to her nose, as she stood there in the hall,
She didn't need to ask from where, she'd smelled that smell before.
"Why is it that,"she muttered, as to the kitchen ran,
"It's only when you're not around, that milk boils in a pan!"

"I've got no socks!" a small voice cried, "and I can't find my tie!"
The mess upon the cooker top had burnt on hard and dry.
The steam ran down the windows and the kettle whistled on.
"Your socks are on the landing floor."
"They're not - I've looked - they're gone!"
"Have you packed my library book?"
"Is my dinner money in?"
"What's for breakfast?"
"Where's my tie?"
Her head began to spin!

The doorbell rang, then rang again - "Oh, who the heck is that?"
She struggled with the rain-swelled door to free the trapped doormat.

58

"Sign here, love" the postman said, as he stood there in the rain.
Two demands for rates ignored, but here it came again.

She didn't even open it, and put it on the shelf,
And her thoughts about the Council kept discreetly to herself.
She made the tea and, as it brewed, the cornflakes she'd prepare,
Another pan of milk she warmed and move she did not dare.

Breakfast done, she cleared away the dishes, spoons and cups,
Cleaned the burnt milk off the hob, then started washing up.
Around her feet the cat meowed, his fur wet from the rain.
"When you have gone, my lad," she said, "we'll not have one again!"

" 'Can we have a kitten? We'll look after him, you'll see',
But now the novelty's worn off, this cat belongs to me."
Into his dish, she put some food, and milk for him did pour,
And with a cloth, wet paw marks wiped from off the kitchen floor.

She glanced up at the kitchen clock, it was almost half-past eight.
"Clean your teeth and comb your hair - come on, you'll both be late!"
From the cloakroom hooks she took their coats
And placed them on the stairs,
Their shoes from in the kitchen fetched,
Brushed shiny black, both pairs.

"If you don't put those comics down, I'll have them stopped, you'll see -
Desperate Dan takes pride of place in this house, obviously."
She kissed them fondly on the cheek and looked at them with pride,
Well turned-out and smart, she thought, as they both set foot outside.
"Mind the traffic on the road and don't be late back home."
She watched till they were out of sight, then suddenly felt alone.

She closed the door and breathed a sigh and combed her tousled hair,
And picking up her coffee cup, she sank into her chair.

MIDSOMER

I've moved away from my practice in town
To a place in the country I've found.
A beautiful parlour, complete with thatched roof
And close to a quaint cricket ground.
This location will be a challenge to me,
My services put to the test,
But the business looks good, there's a flat up above,
And a well-equipped chapel of rest.

The previous owner's retiring
To a six-bedroom house by the sea.
A fortune he's made from the people he's laid
And he's not yet reached forty-three.
I came down to meet him one week in July
To be sure that my move would be right,
And tales he then told of the plots that unfold
And things that go bump in the night.

"This village is really idyllic,
The sun seems to shine every day.
In truth, it's the same as others I'll name -
Just part of a set, you might say.

Midsomer's a county of many small towns
And here in Ferne Basset, you'll see,
A number of murders have come close to here,
And their despatch was entrusted to me.

A call from Tom Barnaby usually means
There's a need for a coffin or two -
It's never just one - the murders go on,
'Till Barnaby's team solve the clue.

"There's Midsomer Magna and Midsomer Barton,
Fletcher's Cross, Little Worthy and more.
The list it goes on - I've been to each one -
And funerals, I've done by the score.
Folk of all kind in each village you'll find,
And their lives seem to be intertwined.
And most that you meet, when out on the street,
Are acceptable, friendly and kind.

"Old ladies on bikes and vicars on trikes,
Village fétes, vintage cars and a choir,
Riders on horseback, old village halls
And big mansions with open-log fire.
But don't be deceived, for it's firmly believed
In each village, at least once a year
Someone will be murdered by knife, rope or gun
And Barnaby soon will appear.

"In Badger's Drift it started, many years ago -
Gruesome murders, one and all
As gruesome murders go.
A broken neck, a shotgun blast
And death by sword for two.
Three suicides thrown in for luck
And so my business grew.

DC Jones and DC Troy and DC Scott have been
With Barnaby at different times
Upon the murder scene.

No village, the exception - each one has had its day.
At Badgers's Drift they've been there twice,
And the funerals came my way.

"Burntwood Mantle, Finchmere, Deverall, Morten Shallows -
Victims poisoned, burned or stabbed
Or hung on makeshift gallows.
Malhem Cross and Draycott and Midsomer Mere
Have had their share of murders
And villagers in fear.

"But now it's time for me to leave
And spend some leisure time
Away from all these villages, and the endless, violent crime.
The murder count is a hundred and eight
And suicides stand at ten.
Natural causes account for nine
With an unexplained death, now and then.
The future for business is looking quite good,
As the Causton records show.
There's been murders galore in twenty or more,
But there's still twenty places to go."

The business I bought, but I've harboured a thought
In the months since my Midsomer move,
This village, you see, has been Barnaby-free
And no murders for Causton to prove.

Ferne Basset is fine, but may be next in line
For the murders and famed CID.
So, I'll keep wide awake and no chances I'll take
For the next in a box could be me.

THE CHALLENGER

With an arrogant air and a shake of his head,
A smug look ensconced on his face,
The would-be tennis star strutted on court
To challenge our Wimbledon ace.
He'd watched the final on telly,
His impression was not of the best,
His belief in himself - he was top of the shelf -
And today he'd be put to the test.

He'd prepared for this day in a punishing way,
Cut down on his burger and chips.
His trip to the pub for a week he'd give up,
And no doughnuts would pass through his lips.
Three times a week he had practiced,
His partners were chosen to be
A challenging test to make him the best,
Their services all came for free.

Three sets he played with the milkman,
Three sets to love made him gloat,
But the cards they were stacked - the milkman was whacked
From the 5am start on his float.

The young kid next door stacked shelves at a store,
And tennis was far from his mind.
He'd took the day off with a cold and a cough,
But agreed to a match to be kind.

Returning a ball - he was no good at all -
His sneezing he just couldn't stop.
The balls all went past him and into the fence,
And his hankie he'd constantly drop.

The park keeper offered to help him
In his quest to compete with the best,
His job was part-time which suited him fine,
'Cos his Zimmer Frame needed the rest.

An email he fired off to Andy,
And stressed this challenge was vital
To prove he deserved the cash he had earned,
And that coveted Wimbledon title.
Fair dues to him, he agreed to the whim
Of this upstart whose name was unknown.
He'd take up the challenge and put to the test
This affront to his claim on the throne.

A crowd had now gathered to witness the match,
The court in the park well prepared.
The grass had been cut to six inches,
And the net had been stitched and repaired.

Three old age pensioners, a bloke with his dog,
Two kids that had bunked off from school,
A down-at-heel tramp, who was searching the bins
(Who'd be sleeping it off, as a rule),
Lined up outside the wire netting.
Was history soon to be made?
The Wimbledon champion put in his place
In this game that was now to be played.

The challenger crouched to receive the first ball,
Like a coiled spring ready to pounce.
Four balls went past him - he didn't see one -
From the bloke who he thought he could trounce.
The first game was gone, his score it was none,
Undeterred it was his turn to serve.
Six times he threw the ball in the air
But his racquet developed a swerve.
He missed every one - the ball, it had gone,
He was swearing and losing his nerve.

At last he connected, it travelled real fast,
Andy was set and stood tall,
But the shot never reached him, it flew out of court,
And the dog ran away with the ball.
Another game lost, he found to his cost,
That every ball he delivered
Was returned super quick with a deft Murray flick,
Its speed, it increased, and he quivered.

The game it wore on - his confidence gone,
The crowd had gone home for their tea.
His score as before hadn't altered at all,
And he'd lost three sets out of three.

With his shirt soaking wet from the strain and the sweat,
He conceded and shook Murray's hand.
"I don't think I'm ready - at least not just yet -
You're really the best in the land.
I'll go back to the telly and tennis ignore,
And give it a rest for a while.
I'll study some programmes on culture,
And start watching *Jeremy Kyle*!!"

LUCKY ME

I'm not the main attraction
Where women are concerned.
But all's not lost, believe me,
'Cos in this life I've learned
That imperfections need not be
A bachelor life impending.
There's someone out there just for you,
This message I am sending.

My nose is really rather large,
I'm only five foot high.
Though my hair's still black,
It's a bit at the back,
The rest has waved goodbye.
I bite my nails and snore at night;
I get drunk and I smoke.
My breath smells like an ashtray
And I cough and wheeze and croak.

My feet are big and hairy
And nearly always smell.
My belly hangs out of my shirt
And my armpits stink as well.
My runny nose just never stops;
My language, it is choice,
But true love now has come my way;
A beauty, name of Joyce.

She's half my age and gorgeous,
And all that I desire.
With hour-glass shape and flaxen hair,
She sets my loins on fire.
She doesn't care I've lost some teeth
And the rest of them gone yellow;
That I've got no job and keep three dogs
And I don't talk - I bellow!

I thought true love had passed me by.
Not in my wildest dreams
Would some take me as I am,
But I'm so wrong, it seems.

I've only known her for a while -
Last Thursday was the day.
She stood behind me patiently
And sent a wink my way.

In the Postal Office queue, I stood.
She watched me as I signed
The claim form for my *Lotto*
And my jackpot was defined.

So don't despair if you, like me,
Have symptoms shown above -
Find six lucky numbers
And you'll find the key to love.

I'M OFF MY TROLLEY

There's a supermarket trolley
That surely must be mine,
Whenever I go shopping
I get it every time.

It hasn't got my name on it,
It's the same as all the rest,
But it always ends up in my hands
And puts me to the test.

My pound it takes as normal
And freewheels through the door,
Gliding smoothly down the aisle
On the supermarket floor.

It's only when my shopping
Is loaded in its hold
It then decides its taken charge
And strange things then unfold.

The wheels they go all wonky
And, try as hard I might,
When wanting to turn left with it
The stupid thing turns right.

I'm sick of saying sorry
For collisions that it makes;
So far I've knocked down three displays
And a stack of *Jaffa Cakes*.

Black looks galore within the store
From shoppers who can't see
That wonky wheels go where they like,
And aim abuse at me.

I know it isn't funny,
When bending down to find
A loaf of bread from a lower shelf,
And get bunted from behind.

A sideswipe can be just as bad
And a lot of bother cause -
I ran into a woman's leg
And she dropped her *Daddies Sauce.*

The cap shot off the bottle
And made its contents soar -
It sprayed two shoppers blotchy red
And the rest went on the floor.

I was lucky, as it happens,
For no-one really knew
Who had done to who and what
In the melée and to-do.

By now I'd made my exit
Up the aisle right to the top
As a bloke arrived to clean it up
With a bucket and a mop.

When people have a change of mind
On their way around the store,
Why is it they don't take it back
To where it was before?

I was searching in the freezer
For a bag of frozen beans -
I shoved aside a bar of soap
And a pair of denim jeans.

I was asked for my assistance
To reach some goods up high;
A little lady couldn't reach
Although she'd had a try.

While standing on the lower ledge
She'd reached up to shelf four
And twenty tins of dog food
Went rolling on the floor.

We both made good our exit
But, in my hurry, took
A trolley belonging to a bloke
Who was browsing through a book.

It wasn't till the bakery,
When looking in my trolley;
I've never bought the *Sunday Sport*
And realised my folly.

I really think that there should be
A simple way of showing
Just whose trolley belongs to who
And stop my contents growing.

People throw things into mine,
And when I reach the till
There's loads of things I hadn't bought
That show up on my bill.

When eyeing up the checkouts
To find the shortest queue,
I can't decide which one to choose,
And every time I do,

I get it wrong and the queue that's long
Has checked out and departed
And muggins me, still standing there,
Not far from where I started.

I made my way from out the store
The car park sure was busy,
Weaving in and out of cars
With my trolley, I felt dizzy.

Why is it when they're driving
To find a parking space,
These would-be-shoppers blow their horns
And sport an angry face.

Yet when they've found a parking spot
And become a walking shopper
They expect all drivers to behave,
And to treat them right and proper.

My shopping safely in the boot,
The trolley I took back.
Its wheels responding as they should
And keeping right on track.

It took its place within the rank,
My pound coin I'd regain
And I guarantee it'll wait for me
When next I come again.

HOLLYWOOD GREATS

Another name from the hall of fame
And the world of make believe -
Tony Curtis joins the ranks
Of stars for us to grieve.

The latest in a dwindling list
From an era long since past
Who have etched their names as Hollywood greats
And their memories, long will last.

If I turn the page to this bygone age
And the stars of whom I speak -
They launched me into fantasy
At the 'Pictures' once a week.
MGM, Columbia, Universal, RKO,
United Artists, Paramount,
With contract stars on show.
Very few alive today, but in this modern age
On DVD and wide TV the world is still their stage.

Humphrey Bogart, Cary Grant, John Wayne and Joel Mcrae,
Shelley Winters, Barbara Stanwyck, Robert Mitchum, Doris Day,
Stewart Grainger, Frank Sinatra, Rock Hudson, Fred Astaire,
Spencer Tracy, William Holden, Bette Davis, Deborah Kerr,
Gary Cooper, Ginger Rogers, Kirk Douglas, Marlon Brando,
Shirley Temple, Judy Garland, Glenn Ford and Greta Garbo.

Gregory Peck, Jack Lemmon, Bing Crosby, Peter Lawford,
Vivien Leigh, Burt Lancaster, Henry Fonda and Joan Crawford,
Ingrid Bergman, Ava Gardner, Elizabeth Taylor, Rosemary Clooney,
Ray Milland, Montgomery Clift, Jane Wyman, Mickey Rooney.

Broderick Crawford, Steve McQueen, Yul Brynner, Betty Grable,
Rory Calhoun, Vincent Price, Jean Simmons and Clark Gable,
Johnny Weissmuller, Robert Stack, Dean Martin, Danny Kaye,
Richard Boone, June Allyson, Robert Donat, Aldo Ray.

Marilyn Monroe, Rita Hayworth, Bob Hope and Robert Preston,
Susan Hayward, Richard Widmark, George Saunders, Charlton Heston,
Katherine Hepburn, Audie Murphy, Jane Russell, David Niven -
This list of names all come to mind as my memories are driven.

No doubt, in time, a similar theme will chart stars of today
And others from the following years of Hollywood's heyday.
How many names will make it? How many stand the test?
Immortality doesn't come unless you act your best!

I'M A CAN OF BEANS

I'm a can of beans on *Tesco*'s shelf;
I'm three wheels on a pram;
I'm a broken plate from a dinner set;
I'm a jar of strawberry jam!
I'm a flag upon a golf course;
I'm a deck chair on the beach;
I'm a clock that's stopped at half past two;
I'm a shelf that's out of reach!

I'm a Cheshire cat with silly grin;
I'm a dog that's lost its bark;
I'm a note left for the milkman;
I'm a torch beam in the dark!
I'm a pothole in a tarmac road;
I'm a heart about to break;
I'm a string upon a banjo;
I'm a slice of fruity cake!

I'm a sky of blue with dazzling hue;
I'm a Christmas card sent late;
I'm a message in a bottle;
I'm a number on a gate!
I'm an apple that's half-eaten;
I'm a cup of tea gone cold;
I'm a horse that won the Derby;
I'm a ring of shining gold!
I'm a man with verse that just gets worse;
I'm a driver of a tram;
Because of you, I ain't a clue
Who the bloomin' 'eck I am!

GIS A JOB!

Looking back it's plain to see
My choice of job was wrong!
Working hard for many years
For hours and days, so long.

If only I had known it then,
It's very plain to see,
I should have got elected
And become a rich MP.

My mortgage paid and then reclaimed,
And all that breaks gets mended -
No cost to me - it's all for free,
My money worries ended!

Family friends I'd see alright
And find them all a job,
Their wages paid, of course, by me -
Then on my expenses fob!

My hanging baskets paid for,
My boiler I'd replace,
I'd have two wide-screen tellies
And a brand new fireplace.

Antique rugs and Tudor beams,
New windows and new bed,
I'd ditch my Vauxhall Corsa
And a Bentley hire instead!

A Sat Nav I would claim for,
Its use is plain to see.
I'll find my way to take a break
In a cottage by the sea!

A whirlpool bath I fancy,
With toilet seat to match;
My ironing I'd have done for me
And new kitchen built from scratch!

A duck house I would put in place,
When my garden is designed,
And should the water start to leak,
I'll have the pool re-lined.

Queuing at the turnstiles is really not for me.
I'll claim a season ticket and go at five-to-three.

Computer problems sorted,
I'll change it twice a year,
And laser printers I'll have two
And breakdowns, never fear!

If I fancy being naughty
I'll hire a film or two,
And on my new recorder, watch,
The movies classed as blue!

Massage chairs and sofas,
Bath plugs, bulbs and soap.
The list goes on and on and on
But I know that I would cope!

For when I see just what I've got
They're really all for free,
And my handsome wage is mine to spend,
On me - on me - on *me*!

And, if by chance, I get exposed
In a Sunday paper hit,
I'll tell them I am sorry
And pay back just a bit.

"I played within the rules," I'll say!
And, "No, I won't resign!"
(There's lots more cash to come my way
Before election time...)

The public then may well forget,
And give to me their cross,
On the gravy train I'll ride again
And I couldn't give a toss!

eBAY

I'm always searching for bargains
And I find it hard to resist.
My favourite place is on *eBay*
So I trawl every day through their list.

There are things that I've bought and no need for.
There are things I have bid for and lost.
There are things that I've learned that ought to be burnt
And found out too late at my cost.

I bid for a gardener's bargain -
A box full of untitled seeds.
But all that I got when they grew in the pot
Was a crop of untitled weeds.
I wanted a Hollywood movie
That Amazon couldn't supply -
Behold there it was on my *eBay*
At a much reduced price I could buy.
Ninety-nine pence for the movie,
The postage didn't cost much.
When I sat down to view I immediately knew
The soundtrack was dubbed and in Dutch!

A hole in my jumper needed repair
And a Pringle you don't throw away.
Invisible cotton's the answer, you've guessed, I logged on *eBay*.
A 'Buy it Now' deal was an option, delivered by post the next day.
The hole in my jumper would soon disappear,

When the cure in the mail came my way.
My needle was ready and waiting -
From the package a large wooden spool,
No thread could I feel as I handled the reel,
Though I tried very hard like a fool.

I bid for a camouflage jacket -
My bid was the highest and won.
I tried it for size but soon realised
Once more it's for sure I'd been done.
The size, it was right, not loose and not tight.
In truth it's a tailor-made fit,
But I took the thing off in the garden
And try as I may I can't find it.

My next buy had a similar ending -
A full-sized fine-tuned air guitar.
Lessons and plectrum included -
My first step to becoming a star!
The parcel arrived and I opened it up -
I can't believe what I did.
The package inside was turned downside up
And the box came away from the lid.
The contents spilled out on my living room floor
Once more I'd been made look a mug.
A plectrum and book was all that I saw
As they lay on my living room rug.

A second-hand aerial never been used
For my upstairs TV I acquired.
Only one bid, I won for a quid,
And only the cable required.
The pictures alright if the cable's pulled tight
And the aerial's down on the floor.
But if channels I change I've a need to arrange

A hook on the back of the door.
If placed by the telly the picture is poor,
The ghosting is really excess.
A soloist singer takes on a new slant
As a soloist trio, no less.

So it's *eBay* again for the aerial -
Never used - will be near to the truth,
And my TV will be much clearer for me
With an aerial fixed on my roof.

My *eBay* dealings I need to curtail
And change my buy into sell.
These things that I list will never be missed
And a few other items as well.

You know what I mean for you've gone where I've been -
Take a look in your cupboards and see
What once seemed a bargain or really must have
You have got quite a hoard same as me.

The *George Foreman Grill* you used only once
That takes you an age to get clean.
The cost of a loaf that lasts just a day
When the bread maker comes on the scene.

A sandwich maker and wet salad shaker,
A Hoover you hold in your hand,
And making your coffee all creamy and frothy
With that chrome polished gadget so grand.

The rowing machine that's now in the shed,
The exercise bike by its side.
The mandolin slicer is back in its box

And the barbecue is rusting outside.
The ice cream maker and *Teasmade*,
The Fondue set's had its day.
Stop now and think, look under the sink,
It is time they were all on their way.

No doubt I have missed many more on this list -
If you look you will find there are many.
But the truth must be told, these things you were sold,
You will find that you didn't need any.

So log on to *eBay*, get rid of your junk,
It's easy - you'll find there will be
Some fool to bid on your cheap, useless goods
And it's likely that someone is me.

So now I am checking my *eBay* –
I am all on my own at a pound,
I hope it will be a triumph for me,
And a bargain again I have found;
An inflatable dartboard only used once
Will soon be winging its way.
The biddings just ended, I've scored once again
And my dartboard will soon be in play!

HAS ANYONE SEEN MY SNOWMAN?

Has anyone seen my snowman?
I left him on the lawn -
A cheery smile upon his face
From dusk right through till dawn.

It took me hours to make him -
He brightened up my day,
But now he's vanished out of sight
While I have been away.

He's left behind his woolly gloves,
His bobble hat and scarf,
His rolled up brolly's on the grass
And his glasses broke in half.

I didn't get a text from him,
He didn't leave a note,
Just his clothes and carrot nose
And the buttons off his coat.

Perhaps he really didn't like
The changing of the weather,
But his mouth can't talk - his legs won't walk
They're moulded tight together.

Someone must have kidnapped him
He'd never leave this place,
Contentment written in his smile
Etched upon his face.

Ten long years he'd waited
To land on my back lawn.
A million flakes of snowy white
Just waiting to be born.

I'll keep the things he left behind,
For winter's not yet done,
And one cold morning waking up,
I'll find more snow has come.

Again, I'll crawl around the lawn
And from the carpet white,
Create once more my snowman
And take him in at night!

DREAMS

On closing my eyes I see coloured skies,
There are stars and strange shapes all alive.
They twist and they turn in the shape of a worm,
Then collect like bees in a hive.

The bright startling hues of the reds and the blues,
The crimsons, the yellows and greens,
All fade out of view as sleep filters through,
And my brain takes charge of my dreams.

Will it be something new, something false, something true,
Something old, something frightening and cruel?
Subconscious is ready for fantasy flights -
And the mind will supply all the fuel.

The canvas is painted, the stage is all set,
The players await in the wings.
The curtain will rise when the lids of the eyes
Are shut tight - and deep sleep begins.

How can it be that the things that I see,
As the pages of life I flick through,
Contain many things incredibly real -
Mixed up - with things that aren't true!

Personalities change, surroundings look strange,
Situations both complex and grand.
Times of great sorrow, elation and love,
And things that I don't understand!

Visits to places I've not seen for years,
And places where I've never been;
Talking with loved ones whose looks are unreal -
Meeting people that I've never seen.

And why, when I'm fleeing in terror
From a stranger who's wielding a knife -
My legs seem to be tied together
And I can't seem to run for my life!

I have raced through acres of cornfield,
So high I can't see o'er the top.
No cash for the fare on a journey
And turfed off the bus at next stop.

At times in the street, just my shoes on my feet,
My clothes I just do not know where,
But people I see take no notice of me -
And ignore me as though I'm not there.

Where do dreams begin? For when I walk in,
They're already half over it seems,
And near to the end, to wake is the trend -
It could only happen in dreams.

CHANGES

Remember the days when watching TV
Was easy and simple to use;
An On and Off button, a Turn-The-Sound-Up
And a knob for which program to choose.

When a phone in the hall was plugged into the wall
With a bell that would ring loud and clear,
And a voice that was human would answer your call
And no music offended your ear.

When writing a letter or sending a card
When a personal touch was the thing,
And pleasure derived when the postman arrived -
What surprise in his bag would he bring?

With a film in your camera and limited snaps
The viewfinder pressed to your eye,
One simple click of the shutter would yield
Eight snaps with a quality high.

A book with its chapters was tactile,
With covers that tempt you to read.
You could flip to the back if you wanted,
If revealing the end was your need.

A car that won't start is a problem,
But with some mechanical nous
You could mess with the plugs, points and battery
On the drive in front of your house.

On a journey by car, be it local or far,
There are signs you can follow each day.
You could follow a map, or open your trap,
And ask some kind person the way.

Times have moved on and all of these things
Are concepts all brought up to date.
New ways we must learn to adapt to the turn -
But for me, I believe it's too late.

The space for my telly has doubled
From two feet, it's gone up to four.
A forty inch screen, no knobs on the front
And a heavyweight stand on the floor.

I could have it wall hung if I wanted -
It would certainly save me some space,
But with my head tilted back to watch it each day
I'd end up with my neck in a brace.

Now the knobs have all gone - to switch the thing on,
There's a remote that is simple to use.
Fifty-four buttons besides On and Off
And I'm blowed if I know which to choose.

Record live TV - watch films on demand -
Pause broadcasts when they're in full flow.
And still there's loads more that I need to explore -
Just what they all do, I don't know.

There's Swap, Zoom and Root, Repeat and Reboot,
Aspect, Subtitle and Store.
There's Screen, Sleep and Link, and Return (that, I think,
Takes me back where I once was before).

I've got Index and Hold and four colours bold
In Green, Red, Yellow and Blue.
These buttons I'll try - they look good on the eye -
But I'm blowed if I know what they do.

Record, VCR, Text, Status and Home
And a V with a plus coloured red.
I sat down at teatime to watch this TV,
And soon it was time for my bed.

I'd watched fifty channels, and voted on line,
I've ordered three shirts and a tie.
I've paid for a blue film to watch for a week,
And subscribed to the movies on Sky.

My old tape recorder is linked to this set,
Along with a Blue Ray machine,
But getting to grips with this system I've got,
Is a nightmare, you know what I mean?

Remote controls - *three!* - I've got perched on my knee,
And buttons I've got by the score.
My surround sound's disabled, I don't really care -
I just couldn't face any more.

I tried switching on, but the picture stayed blank,
My fingers went white doing that.
I pressed every button as hard as I could,
Then found out the batteries were flat.

My phone's just the same, it's a hell of a game.
My landline's a thing of the past.
I've got a new mobile it handles top speed,
But my fingers won't go very fast.

One simple call is not simple at all
If you chance to press the wrong key.
It brings up an App or a GPS map,
Or loads of things alien to me.

It will tell me the time all over the world
When I bring up the digital clock.
But mine seems to be set, 'cause all that I get
Is the time of the day in Bangkok.

No more the bell ring - a ring tone's the thing -
From Mozart to *Match of the Day*.
I can surf on the net and sometimes I get
A shed load of games I can't play.

I get awful vexed when trying to text -
I'm slow and will never get better.
I've come to the conclusion it's quicker for me
To send it by post in a letter.

The number of times when making a call
When the choice of options arrive -
A recorded voice message says, 'Press one to four',
And sometimes I even have five.

If I choose to hang on, when a long time has gone,
There's a voice that I don't understand.
A call centre call (I think from Nepal)
Or from some far flung foreign land.

I've listened to hours of music,
None which would be of my choice;
Three cheers for the years of the old dial up phone
And the sound of a warm human voice.

I traded my car for a new one -
The scrappage scheme too good to miss.
A brand new car for my old one
And a chance for motoring bliss.

But technology comes with a cost I can see,
As under the bonnet I stare.
There's nothing for me to fix by myself -
It's a specialised dealer repair.

No more the cleaning of sooted-up plugs,
Or the gap in the points to re-set.
Book the car in for the dealer to fix
And a large bill you surely will get.

With my Sat Nav fixed on the windscreen
I set out for a day in Newquay.
With the town name logged in, I was soon to begin
A day in the sun by the sea.

"Turn left," said the voice in a soft silky tone;
Who is she? This girl I can't see.
"Carry on for a mile, then take the first right,"
And I thought, this is easy for me.

"Take the third exit at roundabout -
Advance sixty yards to a junction -
Make a left turn" - it was easy to learn,
It was money well spent for this function.

And so it went on (three hours had gone),
But my journey was soon to be broken.
I took a next left that seemed rather odd -
But the girl in the Sat Nav had spoken.

The road was so narrow, no tarmac in sight,
No room to turn round and go back.
A farmhouse with ducks I could see straight ahead,
At the end of this mud-laden track.

I reversed for a mile, it took quite a while,
To the road I was once on before.
But I couldn't check just what had gone wrong -
The Sat Nav had fell on the floor.

I picked the thing up and stuck it back on,
My journey resumed once again.
Twice more it fell off when the sucker dried out,
It was becoming a bit of a pain.

I finally reached the seaside,
And my love of this gadget soon pales.
The Newquay I see is in Cornwall -
And I wanted the Newquay in Wales!

So it's back in its box in the garage -
My map is spread out on the seat.
I'll travel afar everywhere in my car
With its help and the signs on the street.

I use my computer for email,
It's the way things are done so it seems.
No need for a pad and a pen and a stamp,
The answer to everyone's dreams.

But is it better than posting a letter
That is written with pen in the hand.
When it comes to the sending of greetings,
It's the point that I'm making a stand.

Be it written in elegant hand script,
Or a scrawl - I firmly believe
A personal card is a pleasure to write,
And a pleasure to give and receive.

Printed greetings by email,
By *Moonpig* or *Cards Just 4 You*,
Won't stand on your shelf to be looked at for days -
They will blow on the floor if you do.

I read quite a lot and now I have got
The latest for electronic reading.
The Kindle it's called, but of no use at all,
If it's wood for your fire you are needing.

It's a bit like an Etch-A-Sketch in its design,
With hundreds of books held within.
How can they get all these pages inside -
It's so light and incredibly thin.

I enrolled on the database, chose my first book,
Downloaded and glad that I did.
The prices aren't stable one day to the next,
And my book had increased by a quid.

Engrossed in my reading I reached chapter four,
The pages I turned with delight.
The noise that it made as I turned them
Was authentic and sounded so right.

I read on with the story to the base of the page,
With my finger I flipped to the next,
But to my surprise, in front of my eyes,
Was a page full of strange-looking text.

Alphabetical Soduko it says at the top,
And, try as I may, I can't find
Any meaningful sentence that makes any sense -
I flipped over and left it behind.

But the next page is really no better,
My novel gone, goodness knows where.
I've got a full page of musical notes,
And my feelings plunged deep in despair.

Although I'm assured by people I know
That the Kindle's as good as it looks,
I'll leave it around to gather some dust
And go back to my reading of books.

I spoke of the film and my camera,
But now I'm beginning to see
Maybe I'm wrong and really belong
In this era that's here and for me.

With my digital camera I've been out and about
And photographed people and scenes.
The results are astounding and so full of life -
Much clearer and sharper it seems.

No more the limit of frames on a film,
Unlimited snaps I can take,
And if an event I want to recall
A video film I can make.

No processing wait for the pictures,
I can view them without a delay,
No cost to discard any not-up-to-scratch -
'Delete' and they all go away.

Close Up and Zoom are amazing,
Subjects in detail appear,
Draw in a subject from distance afar
For an image that's close and so clear.

Settings for every occasion,
Flash bulbs a thing of the past,
High-powered batteries that drive all these things
Are easy to change and they last.

With your card taken out of the camera
And inserted into a TV
The pictures you took can be viewed right away
And the fruits of your work you can see.

So I've enrolled for a series of lessons,
I know I have nothing to lose.
With luck they will teach me which settings the best,
And show me which menu to use.

Perhaps I should relax my blindfolded view -
And acknowledge the changes I see.
Take my head out the sand, let my mind understand
Such changes could be good for me.

BELLE OF THE BALL & CHRISTMAS DANCE

Tonight is the night of the dance,
Good times and a lot of romance.
We'll have a good time in surroundings sublime
And it isn't really by chance.
This romantic 'do' where I'm taking you
Has been planned for a long time, you see
And with you by my side, I really can't hide
The pleasure that you bring to me.
We will dress to the nines and all will be fine,
The night and the meal, enjoy all.
With you on my arm I will really be proud -
You will be my belle of the ball.

Let's take a walk in the sun,
You and I would enjoy so much fun.
We could stroll arm in arm,
It would do us no harm,
For my heart, you really have won.
We could find a nice shady spot
If the sun it should get very hot,
Hold each other tight while we're out of sight
And there we could thicken the plot.
We could lie side by side and remember
That Christmas we both can recall,
When invited by chance to a charity dance
And you were my belle of the ball!

HAND IN GLOVE

My fingers have been trodden on,
My thumb is badly torn,
Ignored by all who pass me by,
Bedraggled and forlorn.
Does no one care, can no one see
As I lie here on the street
That, though I might look down and out
Life once for me was sweet.

In contrast to my present plight
On a pavement cold and wet,
With my partner I have travelled wide
And famous people met.
From a factory floor I made it
And reached the dizzy heights;
Garden parties, premiers
And sparkling champagne nights.

First class travel I've enjoyed
In top class limousines;
A stately home to live in
Was the answer to my dreams.
My partner was a handsome man
With a job of high esteem;
His dress sense so immaculate
As chauffeur to the Queen.

Two long years together,
Events throughout the land,
He carried out his duties
And I was close at hand.
But then the parting of the ways
My time was up I knew;
He chose to leave me and begin
A life with someone new.

I had a short relationship -
It lasted but a week
With a footman who decided then
That I was past my peak.
My downward spiral then began;
I was left upon the shelf.
A boot boy took a shine to me
And I couldn't help myself.

No more the smart apartment -
He soon put paid to that -
I lodged with him near a boxing gym
In a seedy basement flat.
By day he mingled with the best
And did what boot boys do;
By night he lived his other life
And took me with him too.

Night clubs, drug dens, pubs and clubs
We would visit frequently
And his part-time job to fund it all
Was night-time burglary.
Two nights ago he forced his way
Into a flat at Maida Vale
With me on hand to help erase
The telling entry trail.

A wealthy tenant soon would have
Her jewels and fur relieved
And credit cards for future use
Were very quickly thieved.
But as we made our exit,
Alarm bells sounded clear
And voices shouting out at us
Increasingly came near.

With speed we raced the darkened road
In panic from the sound,
His grasping hand let go of me
And I tumbled to the ground.
He vanished quickly out of view
And, on his own, took flight,
He didn't care as I fell there
In the darkness of the night.

My fall from grace was now complete
As I lay there in the frost.
What use can be a left-hand glove
When the right-hand glove is lost.
But those who treat me with disdain
May live to rue the day,
Good fortune looked them in the face
And they chose to look away.

For here within my crumpled hand,
From a robbery gone wrong,
Lies a diamond-crusted golden ring -
And it's going for a song!

COMING TO A MIRROR NEAR YOU!

When I look into the mirror
It's very strange to see
The reflection I am looking at
No longer is of me.

Where have I gone? That me I knew,
That face for years I've shown.
Who is it that is staring back -
That face that's not my own.

I recognise a part of me
I see in this reflection
But over time there seems to be
Some changes for detection.

And now I see who once was me
That face that once I had,
Has morphed into someone I know -
I'm looking at my Dad!!

MICHAEL FISH

I listened to the forecast
And winter's on its way.
Heavy snow showers overnight
And more throughout the day;

At least a foot and maybe more
The most we've had for years.
A good thick coat and jumper
And hats pulled over ears.

I've got my wellies ready,
My gloves and scarf stood by,
Some knee-length socks and bobble hat
And a twinkle in my eye.

A chance to roll a ball of snow
Up and down the lawn,
And from this carpet of snow white,
My snowman will be born.

I've got his clothes and carrot nose
And buttons for his coat,
My *Dr Who* scarf, six-foot long,
I'll wrap around his throat.

With his bowler hat and glasses,
And a face that's round and jolly,
His pipe stuck firmly in his mouth
And battered, rolled-up brolly,

He'll be the star attraction
For all who pass him by,
Crafted from a million flakes
That drifted from the sky.

In anticipation of the deluge
That soon would come my way,
I rummaged in the garage
To find my super sleigh.

I've had it now for seven years,
But only used it twice;
Its life spent in a corner
With the spiders and the mice.

The runners have gone rusty,
Since its outing years ago
From dragging on the pavement
In just one inch of snow.

I bought a special shovel -
It's hanging on the wall -
Made of orange plastic
And will be no use at all.

I think it's bio-gradable
The colour's really pale.
One good scoop will see it off
Leaving just the stale.

As daylight failed, the sky was clear
And not a cloud in sight.
I went to bed convinced the snow
Would drift in through the night.

I woke up just gone seven,
The curtains threw back wide
To see the foot of snow that fell,
But as I looked outside

Dismay would spread across my face,
Not a flake fell through the night.
The forecast wrong again it seems -
They never get it right!

I looked and looked, then looked once more,
My hopes are all in vain.
No chance to make a snowman
'Cos it's tipping down with rain.

With my sledge back in the garage,
And my shovel in the bin,
My snowman dreams all shattered,
I recalled that silly grin

When Michael Fish predicted
That no hurricane was due;
Then roofs and chimneys disappeared
When the hurricane came true.

So, if like me, you want to see
A snowman on your lawn,
Listen for the forecast
When they promise 'dry and warm'!

FLOWERS AND VERSE

At this time of year
All we hold dear
Are subject to flowers and verse.

Some say it with roses,
Some say it with song,
Some funny, some tacky (or worse).

But my gift to you
It's plain and it's true
It's a promise to you on this day.

I'll love you forever,
Just as I do now,
I'm so glad it was you came my way!

LIFE AT THE END OF THE ROAD

Looking all around me,
As I await my turn,
The air is thick with acrid smoke
As the bonfire tyres burn.

The electro magnet swings above
And has me in its sight
Soon to clasp me in its jaws
Then lift me to a height.

In this dismal yard I'm not alone
As I approach my fate.
There are others here who just like me
Have passed their Sell-By date.

Pristine condition, shiny new,
Leather seats and chrome,
From assembly line to showroom,
We each would find a home.

Prestigious badges, colour, size,
Each one would play its part
In who would buy and own us,
And where our journeys start.

My dashboard wasn't walnut,
My engine size was small,
Basic needs were all I have -
No luxuries at all.

A family car that seated four
In the low price category.
No leather seats to sink in -
Just cloth and PVC.

So, true to form, I started out
As the shiny acquisition
Of a man and wife with two young kids,
and took up my position.

A modest home and a garage
In suburban town estate,
I served their needs for three good years
And life for me was great.

Seaside trips and shopping,
School runs through the week,
Washed and polished frequently
And kept in tip-top peak.

But a family addition
Would make me obsolete;
A larger car would take my place
And a trade-in would complete.

Not for me a showroom -
Those days, by now, were over.
On a garage forecourt, flanked each side
By a Vauxhall and a Rover.

My value now was in demise,
My paintwork looking tarnished,
Rust spots had been camouflaged
And tyre walls neatly varnished.

A first car for a teenage boy,
My windscreen price was right.
A Lexus took the garage space
And the drive was mine at night.

Gadgets new I'd soon acquire;
Go faster stripes adorn,
A boogie box with thumping base
And a Colonel Bogie horn.

In three short years I travelled miles
With occupants galore,
Sometimes six packed tight within
A space designed for four.

Handbrake turns and raceway burns
And parties on the beach,
My back seat springs were tested
If a bed was out of reach.

The pride and joy of the racing boy
Is a car that's got street cred,
But mine was gone and he moved me on
When my MOT was dead.

A cowboy builder bought me
To use me as a van.
With four new tyres and steering rack
A new life, I began.

My rear seats now not needed,
Just a boarded floor instead;
So part of me, I've left behind
As seating for his shed.

Bricks and blocks and bags of sand
Through my hatchback at the rear,
And, suspension failure from the weight
Increasingly grew near.

Fencing panels, copper pipes
I carried on my roof
Anchored to my body parts -
And my paintwork bears the proof.

I struggled on for eighteen months,
Rough treatment I'd endure,
Till belching smoke each engine stroke
Left me without a cure.

The open road for me now closed,
My price tag now was free.
Collected by the scrapyard crew
Who would make short work of me.

My final thought as the crusher loomed
To produce a metal block
When melted down with all the rest
What new life would unlock.

Perhaps again a motor part
On a model for the rich -
Or the shaft upon a golf club
And a life of putt and pitch.

Who knows what fate awaits us all
And what's in store for me.
Well, hold on tight, 'cos here we go
I'll have to wait and see.

MR TOM

There's a cat at my door,
He's been here before -
I gave him a saucer of milk.
He looks quite bedraggled,
With knots, he is saddled,
His fur has lost all of its silk.

He's a tortoiseshell colour with standy-up tail,
And zigzag stripes on his belly.
His mouth seems to be in a permanent grin,
But his breath tends to be rather smelly.
So just on a whim, I let him come in,
He nuzzled around by my feet.
I gave him some fish in my cereal dish
And the look on his face was a treat.

I gave him a shower - it took half-an-hour -
And brushed his coat 'till it shone.
Behold now revealed a beautiful boy
His name from today's; Mr Tom.
In just a short time, Mr Tom became mine,
My house, he regards as his own.
He likes to retire, stretched out by the fire
And he's helped make my house into home.

A saucer of milk was all that it took,
I got Mr Tom on the cheap,
But I know that he'll be a companion for me,
A good friend and a treasure to keep.

ARE YOU SITTING COMFORTABLY?

You can sing this if you want to,
The tune is rather nice.
The words all rhyme and sound just fine
If you think of three blind mice.

I love pies
I love pies
Medium, large or small - I just love them all.
Chicken and mushroom twice a week,
Steak and kidney, potato and leek.
Tell you the truth I'm a bit of a geek
I love pies
I love pies
I love pies
Medium, large or small - I just love them all.
They do you no good and they make you fat,
There ain't no getting away from that.
If your trying to slim give 'em to the cat -
No more pies.

BAR BAR BARBA

My cousin Archie
Hasn't any hair
Just a bit of bum fluff
Scattered here and there.

He doesn't need a barber
Every week's the same
Just a wash and polish
And he's tidy once again.

JACK N JILL

Jack said to Jill,
"Go on the pill
I really think you oughta
Or else we'll end up with a son
Or possibly a daughter".

"No," said Jill, "I hate the pill,
Instead I think you oughta
Get a grip and have the snip,
'Cos it's something in your water."

FOOD FOR THE ARMY

I bought a leg of pork -
It cost me two pounds ten.
I turned the oven up quite high,
Then turned it down again.

And when it was up, it was up,
And when it was down, it was down,
And when it was cooked for an hour and a half
It had turned a golden brown.

Goodnight children, everywhere!

BIRTHDAY GREETING

May your life be filled with laughter and all your dreams come true.
Let love caress you endlessly and all your skies be blue.
Let sunshine bathe you constantly and keep dark clouds at bay.
May fortune seek you and reward on this, your special day.
Birthdays come and birthdays go with just a year between.
My wish for you this coming year - the best there's ever been!

LOST FOR WORDS!

It's really absurd, when you're lost for a word,
And your poetry grinds to a halt.
With a pen full of ink, you sit and you think
And try to sort out what's at fault.

Could it be that your mind, as you search hard to find
The elusive link to your rhyme,
Is a permanent blank - you're thick as a plank -
And your clock has run out of time.

Why is it that sometimes ideas seem to flow
And rhyming just falls into place.
A poem completed in a short space of time
And your pen can't keep up with the pace.

With a mind that's relaxed, the brain can be taxed,
Ideas never in short supply,
And line after line your poem sounds fine
With rhyming that never runs dry.

Subjects galore, never thought of before,
Are dancing and pleading release.
The story evolves, all couplets are solved
And the word count builds up piece-by-piece.

The ending comes soon, you read and fine tune
Your collection enhanced with your ditty.
But keeping the frame of mind that you're in
Is elusive and hard - more's the pity!

Subjects run dry and as much as you try,
New projects you cannot begin.
The key to the door of your vast rhyming store
Has been turned, and you cannot get in.

Lay your pen down, put your paper aside,
Get on with your life day-to-day;
And soon you will find you can open your mind
And with hundreds of words you can play.

Your repertoire grows (for how long, no one knows),
Express all your feelings in rhyme.
The word block removed, you're riding on high
Until you get stuck the next time!

MERRY CHRISTMAS

I have a list of folks I know
All written in a book,
And every year, at Christmas time,
I take it out and look.
And then it is, I realise
These names in there are part,
Not of the book they're written in,
But etched deep in my heart.

For each name stands for someone
Who has touched my life sometime,
And in that meeting, they've become
The rhythm of my rhyme.

I really feel I am composed
Of each remembered name.
And though you may not be aware
Of feelings quite the same,
My life is so much better
Than it was before you came.

So never think my Christmas card
Is just a mere routine -
A name upon a list for now,
And forgotten in between.
For when I send a Christmas card
That I've addressed to you,
It's because you're truly on that list
That I'm indebted to.

And though I've only known you
For months that number few,
You lift me up and play a part
In shaping things I do.
And, so this year, as Christmas comes
I realise anew,
My darkness now has turned to light
Since the day that I met you.

IN THE REALMS OF
THE HIGHLY UNLIKELY

In the realms of the highly unlikely,
There are things that come to the mind,
Things that are rare and rarely occur,
And really so damned hard to find.

A trip to the doctor's and when you appear,
The receptionist says (with a grin),
"Nice to see you; the doctor is free -
Just knock his door and walk in !"

The dentist that spends ten minutes of time
Looking down in your mouth in his chair,
Looking for something expensive
But, in fact, he can find nothing there.

When your treatment is done and you're paying the bill
At the desk, he appears with a smile;
"Have this on me - the treatment is free,
And I haven't said that for a while".

"Your car's in good nick, no fault can I find,
The best I have seen for its year and its kind;
It's worth a lot more than the *Glass'* guide price
You'll find that my offer is nicer than nice.

"An extra two hundred I'm offering you
On a deal for a four-door - spanking brand new.
We will fill up the tank and pay twelve months' tax,
Insurance comes free, you can drive and relax.

"Our terms are the best, I think you'll agree
Pay back for five years and it's all interest free.
When do you want it? Just give us a date.
We'll deliver it pronto outside your front gate."

It's the final at Wembley, we're in the World Cup,
Brazil are the team we must beat.
Extra time we are playing, the whistle is blown,
And a penalty shoot-out we greet.

Brazil, they go first and lead us by one,
But our turn has the self-same success,
Again and again it's repeated,
Composure is turning to stress.

With the score at ten-all, Brazil on the ball,
Their goalie let fly with his boot.
His shot was so weak, it would not reach the goal,
It travelled four foot and took root!

Our shot stopper stood with the ball at his feet,
The crowd turned their backs to the game,
Then, all in one voice, they were chanting,
And Wembley resounded his name.

Swift as an arrow, the ball left the spot,
Struck the crossbar which gave it a boost,
Bounced up off the goalie and into the net,
And the World Cup had come home to roost!

The crowd were ecstatic, Brazilians were stunned,
Wembley was drowning in cheers,
The World Cup we had won - it's once again ours,
And will be for four coming years.

The Chancellor's making a statement,
More cuts, more rise and more pain,
A dose of the usual to fall on our ears,
It's that April day budget again.
The red box is open, the secrets revealed,
A strange smile he expressed on his face.
No look of despair, it just wasn't there,
Not even a sign or a trace.

Our economy's booming, we've paid all our debts,
Employment is rife and it's full.
The exports abroad outweigh what we buy,
In construction - no longer a lull.
We've had a good year, it's abundantly clear
It is time for your share of the cake.
The tax on your petrol, I'm cutting in half
And this statement I now wish to make.

When tomorrow comes round you'll get more for your pound
From six o'clock prompt you will see,
All goods and services tumble in price,
When both become VAT free.
Five million homes we're planning to build,
We've a surplus of cash to be spent.
These homes will be heated at no extra cost,
And all have a peppercorn rent.

Thousands of builders will get the job done
At the rate of a thousand a week.
Results will be swift, is my promise to you -
They are building the first, as I speak!
MPs' expenses will cease from today
This money's a waste - it's a fact.
I've listened to you and all your complaints,
And now have decided to act.

Austerity cuts have spread to this House,
We must take our responses, like you.
And those that complain and can't stand the pain
Will be told in short shrift what to do.

The high speed rail we've abandoned,
The thirty three billion we'll use
To upgrade the railway we've already got,
And buy some Theresa May shoes.

Nurses galore on hospital wards,
Recruitment begins right away.
And a railway brought back into government hands,
Will make all the high fares fade away.

Electric and gas is out of control,
All profits are going abroad.
And so, from the start of the month coming up,
Foreign ownership put to the sword.

There's a twist to detect in this budget,
As yet maybe not plain to see,
I started my speech at eleven
And not at the usual three.

It's Monday today and not Wednesday,
The first of the month not the tenth,
This budget is short, you may well retort,
And not of its usual length.

But it's really a joke, I'm a jovial bloke,
In my red box again I will delve,
The things I have planned are already in hand
And all will be revealed after twelve...

TECHNOLOGY GONE MAD!

Watching sport on telly, it's very plain to see,
It's gone too far to comprehend, at least it has for me!
Each week it seems a growing trend, new graphics to apply,
Statistics that are meaningless - however hard I try.
Every sport they meddle with, every sport's the same,
Straight forward sports all cluttered up with statistics of the game.

Eleven blokes knock a ball around, the simple game of cricket,
Runs are scored between the stumps, if the ball don't hit the wicket.
Six balls in an over, it's the batsman's job to clout,
Two blokes in white to gauge the light and tell you if you're out!
Bowlers fast and bowlers slow, from each end take their aim,
To uproot the stumps behind him and remove him from the game.
The other ten surround the pitch hoping for a catch.
That sends the batsman on his way and help to win the match.
The game goes on till ten men gone, the last man has to yield,
He's not allowed to play alone and has to leave the field.

The score displayed upon a board, the other side come in
To beat that score by just one more, their task they now begin.
Some games are won, some games are lost, bad judgment sets the tone.
If you miss the ball, you'll score sod all, if your middle stump goes down.
So that's the game of cricket, sit back in the stand -
Enjoy the game and the atmosphere in England's pleasant land.

But it's all a different ball game when featured on TV,
There's twelve balls every over, each catch is times by three.
A team of so-called experts dissecting every ball,
Giving out statistics that really mean sod all.

A cartwheel for us all to see where the batsman knocked the ball,
And coloured dots along the pitch denote the delivery's fall.
A hotspot gadget, when it works - keeps us all confused,
A snicker to listen if contact's made, but findings can't be used.
Comments made by has-beens about the style today,
And how it was in bygone days, when your granddad used to play.
Weather forecasts by the hour and a Hawkeye view display
To prove the ball hit nowt at all, and we knew it anyway!
Adverts to distract us, squeezed in throughout the game,
And if it rains we can watch it all - again - again and again.

Football fares no better, when the game is on TV.
One presenter, a giant screen and the pundits number three.
Commentators work in twos, describing state of play,
Repeating well-worn phrases when there's nothing much to say.
'On the back foot', 'on the front foot', 'step up to the plate',
'Early doors', 'they must regroup' and 'balls arriving late'.
Distracting conversations go on throughout the game,
With solutions to what's needed and who's to take the blame.
Moving players around a screen inside a coloured ring,
With solutions why the game was lost, but doesn't change a thing.
The days of Kenneth Wolstenholme are sadly now long gone,
Just the game in simple terms, and gimmicks there were none!

But 'catchup' is the answer when watching on TV
If I delay my viewing, I can watch what I want
And ignore things I don't want to see.
Skip through the adverts and cut to the chase,
Say goodbye to the pundits and chat,
Watch all the football without any break
Or the bowlers, the ball and the bat.

A FRIEND IN NEED

I've made a friend this winter,
He's took a shine to me.
We're getting closer day-by-day,
It's very plain to see.

The friendship began with a fall of snow
That drifted all around,
And the search for food was desperate
On the sparkling frozen ground.

The table in the garden,
Where all the birds can go,
I kept stocked up with tit bits
And free from falling snow.

A delightful scene throughout the day
From my kitchen window view,
Of birds I've seen and fed all year
And some I've seen are new.

Blackbirds, Starlings, Long-Tailed Tits
And Redwings all appear;
Grateful for the chance to feed
At the worst time of the year.

Nuts and fruit and cereal,
Breadcrumbs, seed and fat
Disappeared with speed in their hour of need
And the heaped pile soon was flat.

Among my many visitors
The Robin rarely came at all,
And a fleeting glance was my only chance
To hear his cheerful call.

With Christmas but a week gone by,
And food left in my store,
Lots of things I'd give to them
All past their 'Best Before'.

Mince pies, turkey, bacon bits,
Chocolate log and fruit,
Christmas cake with icing on
All broken up to suit.

But still the absent Robin -
Perhaps just once a day.
Just what was he looking for
To make him come and stay?

On a twitcher's website then I saw
Some tips on feeding birds,
A list of things to feed them,
And what each of them preferred.

Mealworms are the favourite food
Of Robins (so it said),
So I bought a tub and put some out,
With the crumbled cake and bread.

It wasn't long that my Robin's song
Could be heard throughout the day.
His visits now came thick and fast
As he tucked the worms away.

The snow has long now disappeared
And the search for food has eased,
But Robin knows what's good for him,
And he's very easily pleased.

He doesn't mind when I stand outside
Quite close to watch him eat.
On camera, I have captured him
As he hops around my feet.

His visits are reward for me -
Much pleasure I have found,
Observing him and all his friends
Since the snow fell on the ground.

LIFESPAN

With jib held high up in the air, the steel ball winched up tight,
The brake released, its speed increased on it's maiden downward flight.
The roof, it had no answer to this heavy fearsome weight,
And laths and beams were clearly seen amongst the broken slate.

Before the dust had settled, the ball had swung around,
And chimney pots and guttering came crashing to the ground.
Amidst the crowd of people who had gathered in the street,
An old man stood with cap in-hand, his dog sat by his feet.

His lined face showed emotion and a tear came to his eye,
The kids all watched in wonder, while he thought of days gone by.
Life for him had started here, number four in a terraced row,
Born in a back room up the stairs, some seventy years ago.

Two brothers and a sister, the youngest one of four,
The father that he never saw went missing while at war.
His mother struggled on alone, he'd often heard her say,
'This roof above our heads a must, the rent we have to pay!'

The sound of glass impaired his thoughts, as the window frame gave way,
It sparkled on the pavement, where once he used to play
Hopscotch, Tipcat, Kick The Can - all games that now have gone -
Draw a snake upon your back - his memories lingered on!

School days gone, he started work and things were going fine,
Jenny helping Ma at home and three boys down the mine.
In the old zinc bath, by a blazing fire, at the end of the working day,
One-by-one they'd take their turn to scrub the grime away.

Such was life till marriage came and sent them separate ways,
Jenny first, then Bob was next and then big brother Dave!
Life at home with just the two was never quite the same,
His mother's health was failing, and he partly took the blame.
For early rising, cooking, ironing, housework and the such,
To one whose years were closing in, was really far too much!

The pavement trembled beneath his feet as the gable end crashed down,
And the choking dust lodged in his throat his thoughts did quickly drown.
The bedroom floor had disappeared, and in the room below
A black-lead grate hung out in space, its door swung to and fro!

That same old fire, much comfort gave, on nights long since gone by,
As the doctor fought to save the life of a mother doomed to die.
Frail of heart from a lifetime's work, she had only caught a cold,
But trivial things when one is young, aren't so, when one grows old!

"Why ever don't you marry?" the neighbours used to say,
"A fine hard working man like you - you'll live to rue the day!"
But a wife and kids were not for him, he preferred to live alone,
With a lop-eared stray he'd taken in and given him a home.

His working life came to a close, two brothers he'd survived,
Five good years of leisure time, and then that mail arrived!
A motorway with access roads, it seemed the council planned,
Would take the traffic up the North, and with it take his land.

A comfy place in a sheltered home, with a warden close at call.
Beneath his breath he cursed that crane, and its rampant, swinging ball.
Into the van his belongings went - few things he wished to keep -
A rocking chair, a chiming clock and his bed on which to sleep.

On yellowing photos, framed in glass, his eyes once more did cast,
Then packed them carefully in a box, those memories of the past.
His daily walk took him past the house, and so it was this day
He stood and watched it fall apart, his face it showed dismay.
With downcast heart, he crossed the road to gain a closer view,
And with every step the old man took, the danger nearer grew!

The laden lorry heaved and strained, and above the engine's roar,
The driver never heard his cries, as it knocked him to the floor!
And, so it was, that fateful day, with his dog laid by his side,
His life had turned full circle, and where he'd lived - he died!

ONLY A ROSE

Dormant in winter, untended and drab,
Forgotten when summer has gone.
Its beauty is hidden on long winter days,
A far cry from when the summer sun shone.
But sure as the seasons show signs of change,
And the snow is a thing of the past,
Once again, it will flourish in dazzling array
With blooms that will all summer last.
The pure English rose is a joy to behold,
Its perfume hangs long in the air.
The hazards of winter again overcome
With beauty that none can compare!

NOTHING TO DO?

ডক

I'm here on my own watching telly,
There's nothing that I have to do.
Location, Location, I'm watching
About the best thing I can view.

I've flipped through the channels so many times,
With *Freeview*, that's channels a lot.
My finger is aching from surfing
And the remote's getting rapidly hot.

I've eaten my porridge and drunk up my tea,
Fed the cat and been to the loo.
In just a short while it'll be *Jeremy Kyle*,
So I must find something to do.

As I look out the window I see the front lawn -
It could do with a bit of a mow.
The glass in the window is hazy
And really needs cleaning, I know.

The more that I think of the jobs that require
A bit of care and attention,
The list is enormous and still growing fast,
Much faster than I'd like to mention.

The basket of washing, fresh from the line -
It's been in there for almost a week
Waiting for someone to plug in the iron
(And that someone is me, so to speak).

The car needs a wash, the carpet needs vaccing,
Two shirts I have got, but a button they're lacking.
I found six odd socks on their own in a drawer
But somewhere in there's another six more.

My wardrobe is full of clothes I don't wear
And don't even fit anymore.
It's time they were sorted as clothes that I want -
And the rest of them - out of the door.

The living room light is three-quarters efficient,
No light from bulb number four.
Fitting a new one won't do any harm,
And will make things as bright as before.

The garden display I've enjoyed every day
Full of plants that I grew on from seed.
In the greenhouse, there's lots of trays and clay pots
And a really good scrubbing they need.

There are things in the loft that need sorting,
Many things have been up there for years.
Action Man lives on forever,
Along with his friend, *Tiny Tears*;

Photograph albums, old birthday cards,
And things that, perhaps, I could sell.
Long playing records, old 45s
And a *Dansette* player as well.

Out-of-date cameras and printers
And tools I don't need any more.
Boxes and bags of goodness knows what
Lie scattered around on the floor.

The video recorder's a thing of the past,
But my films on cassette all live on.
I'll need a few hours to sort them all out
But I'll have lots more space when they're gone.

My hardback library has filled all the shelves,
And reading them twice is a doubt.
An *Amazon* list I need to compile
And clear the whole lot of them out.

The CD collection needs urgent attention -
The DVD choice is the same.
Alphabetical order they all used to be
And easy to search for a name.

I could spend the whole day just sorting the shed -
I kept stuff I might need any day.
Truth is, it's junk and will never get used
And I should have chucked it away.

My mind is awash with these jobs that I have,
My list I now need to review.
So I'll sit here awhile, watch *Jeremy Kyle*,
And decide which one first I will do!

OUR VALENTINE

The wind blows cold, the night is black,
There's a sparkle of frost on the ground.
The trees lost their leaves a long time ago,
And there's not a spring bloom to be found.

Soon comes the snow; with temperatures low,
The wildlife is searching for food.
Only the evergreens stand up and fight,
When winter is in a bad mood.

The icicles hang like glistening spires
From the rooftops of buildings and trees.
Their branches sag with the weight of the snow,
And fish swim deep or they freeze!

With curtains drawn tight to keep out the night,
The houses are dens of desire.
The winter forgotten with oceans of tea,
Hot soup and a chair by the fire.

All through the night till dawn of first light,
The snowflakes are borne on the wind.
The mantle of white is a wonderful sight,
But the cold shows no sign of rescind.

Animal tracks can be seen in the snow,
The fox scathes a trail with his brush.
Bird tables visited time after time
By Sparrow, Robin and Thrush.

Only the strong survive winter's grip
To emerge with the warmth of the sun.
Each year there are victims of life's yearly trim,
And has been, since time begun!

Under the blanket of sparkling white
Lies a beauty that's dormant till spring.
A bloom that will flourish with fragrance divine
And delight, with its colours, will bring.

All that it needs to survive year-to-year
To grow stronger and stronger each day
Is love and attention, when needed at times
And forever, its blooms will display!

Through ages of time, this beauty divine,
Belongs like a hand in a glove.
It's abundantly clear on this date each year
It's a token of undying love!

For everyone knows that the pure English rose
Is a symbol of heart, mind and deed.
Its thorns are the hazards we all face in life
And its blossom, the love we all need!

My Valentine sweetheart, I love you so much,
Like the rose, you have grown to mature.
As Valentines go, you're my rose in the snow,
Of this, you can always be sure.

REFLECTION

Looking back throughout the years
I've encountered in my past,
So many things have happened
And the changes, they are vast.
It is my belief that in those years
Of three score years and ten,
Such rapid change in such short time
Will not be seen again.
Many things are here to stay
And be improved upon -
Other things have had their time
And they have come and gone.

A six-year war, the London blitz
And years of food on ration;
The rock and roll craze came about
And Teddy boys were in fashion.
The Berlin wall constructed; the Berlin wall took down.
The steam train and the miles of track
That linked most every town.
Coal mines closed - shipbuilding ceased
And soon put to the sword.
A swathe of home-built motor cars -
And production went abroad.

Recording programmes from TV
Was really something new
With Betamax and VHS,
The trend so quickly grew.

But the video recorder's birth and subsequent demise
Would last for only twenty years
When digital arrives.
Sir Edmund Hilary led the way
To end man's awesome quest,
And plant the flag of England
On top of Everest.

Agatha Christie's *Mouse Trap*'s about to reach an age
Of sixty years without a break upon the London stage.
The longest reign of Monarch that England's ever seen
Achieved since 1952 when Elizabeth became Queen.
Yuri Gagarin staked his claim,
First in the human race,
To leave the bounds of Mother Earth
And venture into space.
Following in his footsteps,
America very soon
Sent Neil Armstrong on his way
To step out on the moon.

Many more would tread his path -
The Apollo launchings grew,
Replaced in 1981 with developments anew.
Flying at the speed of sound,
Concorde reigned supreme,
'Till running costs and tragedy
Were soon to end the dream.
The USA would lead the way,
A structure built in space
To orbit round the universe
For astronauts to grace.

The shuttle came and conquered,
But now its time has gone -
Its final flight completed
No more to carry on.
It takes its place in the race for space,
On show for all to see
The achievements made by all concerned
In manned flight history.

On a far-off shore, we went to war,
The Falklands to defend -
Defeat for Argentina
And in three months, it would end.
The first heart transplant, the birth pill,
The first four-minute mile;
The World Cup won in Sixty Six
Would make all England smile.

The three-day week, the miner's strike,
The Winter of Discontent;
The bubble car - the *Sinclair Five*,
Both soon came and went.
Influential people who passed this way in time,
Whose names remain for good or bad in politics or crime.
Some in entertainment, in film or on the stage,
Some with their inventions - all entered on the page.

The list of names, far from complete
Are really just a few
Whose names will be remembered
And listed in *Who's Who*.
Saddam Hussain, Gadaffi, Mussolini and Pol Pot,
Adolph Hitler heads the list -
All men who lost the plot.

In a lighter vein, it's hard to name
All those who passed this way,
And made a lasting memory
In our lives we lead today.
Winston Churchill, JFK (whose deeds much change would bring),
Aneurin Bevan, Christian Barnard, Martin Luther King.
Margaret Thatcher, Tony Blair, George Bush - in later days,
Would leave their mark as leaders,
With their controversial ways.

Music styles are many and in this bygone age
Are singers who can still hold forth -
Though long have left the stage.
Bill Haley brought us rock and roll - his music paved the way
For a dance craze that would sweep the world
And still stands good today.
Elvis Presley came along
And soon was Number One -
He may have left the building,
But his music still lives on.

Frank Sinatra, Nat King Cole, Dean Martin, Buddy Holly;
Ella Fitzgerald, Peggy Lee, Lois Armstrong, Pavarotti
All entered in the hall of fame
These names are here to stay,
Along with new inventions
That shape our lives today.
The Comet jet plane introduced
The chance to see the world.
A maiden flight to Johannesburg
Would see those flights unfurled.

From Watford through to Rugby in 1959
The M1 motorway was built
And shortened travelling time.

Credit cards and *Velcro*, the automatic door,
Tupperware and *Super Glue*, the first self-service store.
Television, ITV, the pocket calculator,
The CD disc, the home PC -
The iPod followed later.

The helicopter lifted off, the hovercraft took to sea.
Ken and *Barbie* both were born and colour for TV.
Digital camera, digital watch and digital recorders,
Plasma screens and LCD and pizza, made to order.
KFC, *McDonalds* and Chinese takeaway,
Along with curry houses are open, night and day.
Pictures for the first time, through space from planet Mars,
Dual control for learners and air bags in our cars.

Microwaves and cash machines, *Windows* for PC,
Clockwork radio, Internet and DVDs to see.
The world-wide web and e-mail, Sat Nav, the ring pull can,
Inkjet printers, mobile phones, soft ice cream from a van.
Remote control and barcodes, *Pot Noodle* and The Pill,
Roller blades and *Tipp-Ex* and George Foreman's *Super Grill*.
Aerosols and *Scrabble*, satellite TV,
AstroTurf, *Viagra* - all here for you and me.

And finally. here's just a few of the landmarks we can see
That could, in time, become a part of England's history.
The Channel Tunnel, The London Eye, the Angel of the North,
Wembley Stadium, the Olympic Village and Canary Wharf.
The Eden Project, The 02 Dome, the Barrier on the Thames,
The Shard of Glass near London Bridge, which when construction ends
Will stand as Europe's tallest - reaching to the sky,
In excess of a thousand feet and eighty storeys high.
In years to come - I may be wrong - for as discoveries go,
Just what surprises come in life - we really do not know.

THE TIMES, THEY ARE A' CHANGING

The high street scene we used to know
Has changed beyond belief.
Famous names have disappeared,
And many come to grief.

Empty shops, some boarded up
Are seen in every town,
And names we took for granted
Are gone or closing down.

Perhaps the biggest change, so far
In the high street that we knew,
Was the *Woolworth* chain that folded
As the list so quickly grew.

One by one these shops have gone,
And it's sometimes hard to see,
Just how many names we know
And now, they cease to be.

Do It All and *Focus, Tandy, T J Hughes,*
Foster Clothes and *Etam, John Collier, Saxone Shoes.*
Ottakas, John Menzies, Safeway, C&A,
Fine Fare, Past Times, Richard Shops, Allders, Comet, Gateway.
Dolland & Aitchison, Midland Bank, Dewhursts, Vision Hire,
Granada, Dixons, Unwins Wines and *Adams* kids' attire.

MFI, Ethel Austin, Lunn Poly, Littlewoods,
Rackhams, Rosebys, Beatties and *Salisbury Leather Goods,*
Freeman Hardy Willis, The Virgin Megastore,
Radio Rentals led the way - and soon there followed more.

Ratners, Timpsons, Sketchley, long gone *Timothy Whites,*
Bejam, Finlays, Habitat, while closure *Peacocks* fights.
Ponden Mill and *Borders, Kwik Save, Owen Owen,*
Threshers, Milletts, Somerfields - and still, the list keeps growing.

The footfall in the high street has fallen day by day,
As retail parks attract us all and lure our trade their way.
Inviting, warm and sheltered, these places seem to be,
With easy access car parks, and most of them are free.

When trading stops in high street shops
And the shutters all roll down,
It brings an air of sad despair in city or in town.

New names are quickly needed to fill the trading gap
And keep the custom in the shops
And the town still on the map.

Charity shops, to some extent, are helping with the trend -
They're mixing in with traders new
In the high street's modern blend.

These changes now have started, new ventures start to spread,
Replacing names in every town with their own brand names instead.

The House of Fraser, Primark, New Look and *Monsoon*
And spreading out like wildfire, the *Mobile Phone* shop boom.
The *Car Phone Warehouse, Vodaphone, Talk Talk* and *O2,*
Virgin Mobile, Telecom, Orange, Phones 4U.

Costa Coffee, B&M, Subway, Dominoes,
The *Firework Shop* that's seasonal and quickly comes and goes.
Pret-A-Manger, Maplins, Apple, Next and *Game,*
Claires, Specsavers and *The Works* - and all towns look the same.

Poundland started up a trend
For a low-priced bargain store,
And copycat shops soon followed,
Increasing more and more.

These changes are upon us now,
But still there's more to come.
The internet is gaining pace
As more buy online is done.

These changes we are seeing in everybody's town
Are the changes that can change again
And bring the shutters down.

TELLY'T AS IT IS!

Remember when the telly
Was plain and fancy free,
A simple knob to turn it on
And watch the *BBC*.

A Volume and a Contrast knob
To make your viewing bright
And a slide control stopped
Pictures from slipping out of sight.

To switch it on or turn it off
You'd get up off your bum.
No lazy way with remote control,
For they were yet to come.

In black and white 'till eleven at night,
When closedown was the norm,
This simple set was soon to be
The calm before the storm.

Commercial telly came our way,
A new set then required,
With bigger screens and handsets -
Your old TV retired.

New programmes, new announcers,
Game shows and the soaps,
Commercial breaks you might not like,
But still you had to cope.

The *Beeb* took up the challenge
With another service new -
Another station on your set
And called it *Channel Two*.

Improvements to your picture
To lines of six two five
Would make your set once more defunct,
And a new one soon arrive.

Just when you thought that this TV
Would be a set to last,
Along came coloured telly
And its sell-by date was past.

A seventeen inch or twenty one
(the biggest one they do)
In colours bright to watch each night -
The choice was up to you.

A rapid rise in channels
That we could watch for free,
Channel Four and *Channel Five*
And more from *ITV*.

Things now seemed so out of hand,
No more your home TV.
Electronic lessons sure would help
Or perhaps a First degree.

Pay TV then came along,
And channels, by the score.
Then *Cable*, *Sky* and *Freeview*
And hand controls galore.

Hanging proud upon your wall
Another telly found,
With plasma screen of giant size -
Complete with surround sound.

Camera and computer slots,
Printer ports as well,
With button red that you can press
To vote or buy and sell.

The AV button is the key
To all these wondrous things,
With many more to come I'm sure,
Just waiting in the wings.

Don't think now that it's ended,
And this telly is your last,
For very soon, believe me,
Its day will soon be past.

A superseded version,
With gadgets shiny new,
Will soon emerge upon the scene
That require new tellies, too.

So save your money - be prepared
For the launch of 3D day.
Once more old models out the door,
'Cos the new one's on its way.

SEASONAL REFLECTIONS

How easy, in the midst of Spring, when all around is green
To cast away the months pre-May as though they'd never been.

The hours of daylight, chirping birds, the blossom on the tree,
Annual holidays getting near, the sand, the dunes, the sea.

With whites well-pressed and bats well-oiled, the cricketers appear;
Bending legs and stretching muscles, dormant since last year.

Fledglings flutter from tree-to-tree to learn the art of flight,
The sun hangs long in painted skies holding back the night.

The sound of the mower with its keen-edged blades trundles to and fro,
Weaving a pattern of shaded stripes, as the grass is scythed down low.

The long awaited fall of rain from silver edged-dark cloud
Releases the smell like the dank from a well on the parched and dusty ground.

Droning bees with yellow knees flit from bloom-to-bloom,
A pleasant, yet a warning sound, when listening to their tune.

With drunken flight the butterflies pass, it seems they never know
Where they've come from, where they are, or where they want to go.

The silver jets glint in the sky and leave their billowing trails,
Ferrying passengers across the sea to lands where sun never fails.

On tarmac roads in the heat of the day, an illusion, a mirage appears,
Glistening waters like silvery lakes that vanish whenever one nears.

There are joggers and hikers and once-a-year bikers
Entranced by the call of the sun.
The blisters are part of this sporting art,
It's healthy, it's slimming, it's fun.

There's greenhouse tomatoes with a taste of their own,
There's strawberries for picking for pleasure.
There are roses, barbecues, suntans and picnics,
All joys in the sun we can treasure.

The list is unending, we all have our thoughts
Of the good things the summer months bring.
But cast your mind back, as you laze in the sun,
To the months that led up to spring.

Let us go back to November and
Recall things we'd like to forget;
It's seven a.m. in the morning,
It's foggy, it's cold and it's wet.

Time to get up, but loathe to get out
From the cosy warm sheets of the bed.
The room is in darkness, you know you must rise,
But you wish you could lie there instead.

At the bus stop you wait, but they're all running late,
And the cold bites your fingers and toes.
Driving's a nightmare in dense, swirling fog
And you hope and pray it soon goes.

On to December, the ice and the snow,
The frost and the early, dark nights.
Your fuel bills will rise and your money demise
With the use of the gas and your lights.

Your mail will be late, for your milk you must wait
When the roads are all covered with snow.
The wheels they are willing, alas they keep spinning,
And try as they may, they won't go.

The New Year arrives and colder it gets,
The frost can be seen at its worst.
Your car just won't start and it fair breaks your heart,
When you find that your plumbing has burst.

The days linger on and you wish winter gone
And you long for the months far ahead.
But don't get despondent, forget all these things,
And think of the good things instead.

All's not as bad as it's painted,
There's beauty, excitement and fun.
The kids have a ball when snow starts to fall,
And don't give a jot for the sun.

There's beauty abound on snow-covered ground
When the trees wear their mantle of white,
And what can compare, as you stand and you stare,
At the stars on a clear winter's night?

Excitement at Christmas for the young and the old,
It's a time that is so full of joy;
The parties, the presents, the tree decked with lights,
The music, and kids with their toys.

The New Year's party with family and friends,
Fresh hopes and good wishes expressed.
The Old year has gone and the New one begun,
Resolutions are put to the test.

Bargains galore, you can buy from the store,
If you stand in the queue at the sales.
Warm coats and umbrellas are bargains indeed,
Cause you'll need them in March for the gales.

The days they grow longer, the birds build their nests,
The grass on the lawn starts to grow.
Already forgotten, the icy cold winds,
The frost, the fog and the snow.

The year's turned full circle; it's where we began,
The buds appear on the trees;
It's spring-time once more; there's good things galore,
So don't be so damned hard to please!

WHO WANTS MY VOTE?

The election is upon us
And change is on its way;
Whichever party wins it
Will do this and that they say.

Healthcare, education, transport to the fore,
Followed then by climate change
And plans to help the poor.
Student fees, security, immigration rules,
Banker's bonus, hospitals
And change within our schools.
Single mums, and tax breaks, prisons, VAT.
These things would seem, with new regime,
Change for you and me.

I know they're all important,
But what I'm looking for
Is a party pledge to alter things,
And quickly pass a law
To put an end to a growing trend
And the increase to us all,
Of annoying things we all endure,
And make their numbers fall.

So here's a list of things to do
For a budding new MP;
Campaign their change or re-arrange
And you'll get a vote from me.

When I buy a daily paper
To read the latest news,
I'm sick and tired of inserts
That tumble on my shoes.

My biscuit packet clearly states
'To open, please pull here'
But the tag is hidden, stuck down tight
And often nowhere near.

Loo roll perforations that only go halfway
Are twinned with kitchen towelling
To while away your day.
Rolling up the excess that's wrapped around your feet
While, in your hand, the torn remains
Of a ragged half a sheet.

A new CD can really be
Sweet music to the ears.
But taking off its overcoat
Reduces me to tears.
There is no tag to tear it off,
Its edges all well sealed.
The shrink wrap films resilient
And never wants to yield.
The only way to save the day
And end this futile strife
Is to let your nails grow long and sharp
Or use a *Stanley* knife.

At breakfast time I have a choice
Of cereals to eat;
Cornflakes, porridge, muesli,
Shreddies or *Puffed Wheat*.

No matter which one I decide
Will be my choice today,
The exasperating problem comes
When I put the box away.

The inner bag I roll down tight
To keep the contents dry,
But the plastic seems elastic,
And (no matter how I try),

It rolls back up and opens
And my temper's surely taxed -
It never used to be this way
When the paper used was waxed.

But worst of all is *Weetabix*
In its shiny silver sleeve,
Whose contents crumble easily
When trying to retrieve.

The packet will not open
Without a forceful tear,
Then loads of crumpled *Weetabix*
Are scattered everywhere.

When eating out in restaurants
And ordering the fish,
The tartar sauce and vinegar
Are usually in a dish,

Enclosed within a sachet,
But, when the corner's torn,
Half of it goes on your plate -
And the rest of it is worn.

Sellotape upon a roll
Can fix a host of things,
But if you lose the end, you'll go round the bend
With the problem that it brings.

You can twirl it round for ages
As you seek the tape's beginning.
With a bit of luck, your nails will pluck
And you think at last you're winning.

But the general trend of this elusive end
Is to wind up when it rips
With two inch lengths with pointed ends
And a lack of full width strips.

Biscuit packets all should state
In letters clear and bold,
Their dunking time in cups of tea
And just how long to hold.

There's nothing more annoying
When your biscuit breaks too soon,
Than the aimless search for a submerged piece
And retrieve it with a spoon.

Dripping teapots, that would seem
In most department store,
Are always paired with milk jugs
That simply will not pour.

Along with wobbly tables
That make your teacup spill,
They need a place mat under them
To keep the damned thing still.

Milk in *Tetra* cartons, bubble packs galore,
Sweet bags tearing top-to-tail
Spill contents on the floor.
Childproof caps and ring-pull cans,
Bottle tops too tight,
The list goes on and on and on
And all need putting right.

A little thought is all it needs
To make most things seem better,
Think back to queues of six or more
When trying to post a letter.

Eyeing up their numbers,
You jumped from queue to queue,
Then find the teller off to lunch
When the next in line was you.

The snaking line and barrier tapes
Have proved without a doubt,
That simple problems can be cured
And most things sorted out.

So, if like me, you want to see
Some changes next election,
Compile a list and add to mine -
It's a vote in the right direction!

I WILL RETURN

Some say there's life after death,
And should that really be
I know the life I would choose
And that's the life for me.

I'd come back here and be a cat
If my life I lived again,
As long as I could find a house
Like mine here in this lane.

The feline friends that live here,
I've had them both for years.
I don't own them - they own me -
At least that so appears.

Never do they have to work
To help pay for their keep.
They're both retired and all required
Is a place to eat and sleep.

A cosy bed for both of them
Hung on a radiator,
Free from draught, both front and aft,
And a daytime bed for later.

Food supplied, both wet and dried,
In varieties galore:
Chicken, beef and choice of fish,
Each week it seems there's more.

Cat pills, vet bills, toys and treats,
They both get this for free.
Scratch post, catnip, and the rest,
They're all supplied by me.

They sleep and play throughout the day
And when I watch TV,
They stretch out by an open fire,
Or curl up on my knee.

First in line at breakfast time,
Lunchtime, dinner too,
A loud *meow* says, 'feed me now'
And that's just what I do.

Affection and companionship is all I'd have to give
In my second life, should I come back
It's here I'd want to live.

A DREAM OF CHRISTMAS

My dream of Christmas takes me back
To a time long since gone by,
To the era of Dickens and *Oliver Twist*
I'll go back if I can - least, I'll try.
The pictures painted in films that we see
Of the Christmas of long, long ago,
Conjure up scenes that were magic it seems,
That perhaps in real life wasn't so!
It snows without fail every Christmas Eve,
The trees wear a mantle of white.
The hand-painted signs swing over each shop,
Their goods lit by soft yellow light.

The cozy red glow of a brazier fire,
Roast chestnut aromas abound.
With fingerless gloves, they're put into bags
And the kids, for a warm, gather round.
The old cobbled street, now inches in snow
Is a picture of life and delight.
Sleighs drawn by horses with jingling bells
And lanterns that twinkle at night.

The toy shop is full of handcrafted goods,
Tin soldiers line up on parade.
The rag dolls look down from their shelf on the wall,
And the owner's akin to his trade.
A genial man with a permanent smile,
His cheeks ruddy red as a rose,
With white tousled hair and a pair of half specs
Perched down on the bridge of his nose.

Out on the street, with snow round their feet,
The carollers wend on their way,
With lanterns held high in the snow-laden sky,
They sing for pleasure, not pay!

Inviting is the word for feelings incurred,
As the windows of houses I pass.
The roaring log fire burns bright in the grate,
Reflecting the flames in the glass.

The paper chains dance on a current of air,
Their shadows are dancing in tune.
The Christmas tree candles flicker and wave,
Such a feeling of warmth in the room.

Large presents are placed at the foot of the tree,
With wrappings excitingly bright.
The grandfather clock ticks loud in the hall,
And the kids are tucked up for the night.

In just a few hours, when daylight appears,
The spirit of Christmas is here;
The presents, the toys, the love and the joys,
It is truly the best time of year.

The church bells ring out, the people file in,
The choir boys are all in fine voice.
His birthday remembered, in songs of high praise
In the spirit of Christmas, rejoice.

But this scene that I've set is as close as I'll get
To that Christmas of long, long ago,
For times they move on, alas, they have gone -
Just melted away like the snow!

WHAT HAVE YOU DONE?

I've woke up and smelled the coffee
I've stepped up to the plate
I've pushed a lot of envelopes
I've learned to love not hate

I've had my share of sorrows
I've thanked my lucky stars
I've made my bed and laid in it
I've gone in no holds barred

I've put my best foot forward
I've trod where angels fear to tread
I've lived the life of Riley
I've woken up the dead

I've taken things for granted
I've learned from my mistakes
I've dreamed the dream
I've reigned supreme
I've put icing on the cakes

I've been unsparing with the truth
I've told the odd white lie
I've burned the candle from both ends
I've been hung out to dry

I've diced with death a time or two
I've been to hell and back
I've kept a secret to myself
I've put life back on track

I've looked through rose-tinted glasses
I've gone beyond the pale
I've chanced my arm and rode my luck
I've lived to tell the tale

I've had my fingers burned
I've lived and learned
I've always pulled my weight
I've done my best with every test
I've had lots on my plate

I've counted the cost
I've loved and lost
I've lived to rue the day
I've stood up tall
I've been made to look small
I've had things my own way

I've been brave and strong
I've bit my tongue
I've sometimes lost the plot
I've thrown my hat into the ring
I've give thanks for what I've got

I've seen the other side of things
I've admitted I was wrong
I've changed my tune
I've been over the moon
I've sung a different song

I've been cruel to be kind
I've lost my mind
I've gone to the back of the queue
I've bet my bottom dollar
I've started over anew

I've took advice
I've paid the price
I've never had it so good
I've lived and let live
I've give all I could give
I've sorted the trees from the wood

I've been not like me
I've barked up the wrong tree
I've spoken out of turn
I've played by the rules
I've not suffered fools
I've had to live and learn

I've won the argument
I've lost the race
I've been told just where to go
I've learned that size don't matter
I've took a body blow

I've been put in my place
I've had egg on my face
I've been cut down to size once or twice
I've been lucky in love
I've worked hand in glove
I've been quite naughty but nice

I've stuck to the plan
I've carried the can
I've made matters worse, it's been said
I've been ill-at-ease
I've been down on my knees
I've never spoke ill of the dead

I've took many a chance
I've led someone a dance
I've wasted somebody's time
I've slung my hook
I've been read like a book
I've seen no reason or rhyme

I've been at a loss
I've not given a toss
I've given a leg a good pull
I've phoned a friend
I've got there in the end
I've lived my life to the full!

DOWN BUT NOT OUT

There's a guy down our street with wings on his feet,
His missus has born him a boy.
A dad he now is and he's all in a tizz,
Full with pride, satisfaction and joy.
He's only been wed for a couple of months,
His romance achieved super quick.
He met his beloved the day she came out
From the sentence she'd served in the nick.

In the café, she sat in the corner,
Her belongings wrapped up on the floor.
He clocked her as special, his heart skipped a beat
The minute he walked through the door.
"Can I sit at your table?" he asked with a smile.
"No problem," she politely replied.
"I'm here all alone, I ain't got no home,
I've spent the last six months inside!"

Undeterred by the fact that she'd been in the jug,
His ardour was reaching its peak.
He'd not had the pleasure of love, he recalled,
Since twelve months on Thursday last week.
She looked a real treat as she perched on her seat,
Though her hair was a bit of a mess.
The nicotine stain on her fingers was dense,
And the crumbs off her cake, down her dress.

"Let me get you a soup and a fresh cup of tea,
Then we'll go for a walk, if you like.
I'll sit facing the window, 'cos I ain't got a lock on me bike."
They chatted a while, she gave him a smile,
The waitress appeared with the bill.
He opened his wallet and gave her a tenner,
the notes that were left numbered nil!

"If you've no place to go, I'd like you to know
You are welcome to stay in my flat.
It ain't nothin' special, there's only one bed,
But I'm sure we can get over that!"
A look of acceptance took over her face,
His offer she really did like;
Then while they were looking in each other's eyes
Some bloke rode off with his bike!

"You can't trust anyone living round here,
They'd pinch the milk out your tea.
I hope he falls off, 'cos the brakes they don't work -
I know, 'cos it happened to me!"
On the way to his flat, as they walked hand-in-hand,
He stopped and took off his shoe.
The cardboard insole, cut down to size,
worn out with his sock poking through.

"My benefit payment is due to arrive,
Next month it's due to go up.
I've ordered a new 3D telly;
I need it to watch the World Cup."
The door to the flat was a sickly light green,
The letterbox jammed open wide.
The junk on the floor that was pushed through the door
He sorted when they stepped inside.

The benefit cheque he quickly retrieved,
And the rest were left on the floor.
Some were for payments of things on the knock
And these he chose to ignore.

The living room stank of tobacco,
The ceiling was stained from the smoke.
Two chairs and a table, a big flat screen telly
And signs of a pig in a poke.
A worn out settee with cushions askew,
Crisp bags screwed up on the floor.
An ashtray in need of attention;
It just couldn't hold any more.

A pair of old jeans hung over the table,
A dirty stained T-shirt beside.
All around there was clutter,
Some stale bread and butter,
And a mug of cold tea by its side.
The carpet and curtains were way past their best,
The paper hung loose on the wall.
But among all this mess an American fridge
Brand new and about six foot tall.

No sign on her face of this utter disgrace,
She followed him out of the room
Into the kitchen that quickly revealed
Chaos, squalor and gloom.
A sink full of saucepans, dishes and cups,
A draining board full of the same.
A grease-laden cooker, stains on the floor,
And the smell of an unhealthy drain.

She cast her eyes 'round the bedroom,
Clothes strewn down on the floor.
Bedclothes abandoned, left in a heap,
A dartboard hung up on the door.
A wall-mounted telly dwarfed the one wall,
An Xbox with games on a shelf.
She thought for a while then gave a half-smile,
This reminded her most of herself.

Thrown out of home by her parents,
A teenager gone off the rails.
Her self-destruct attitude inevitably led
To a sentence in two county jails.
Drug dealing, shoplifting, breeches of peace,
Court orders for all you could name.
From a one-bedroom hovel she reached a new low,
And took to a life on the game.

"I think it is time for both you and me
To take stock of just where we are.
Life is a journey and should be enjoyed,
And we've both not got very far.
Let us discuss our needs and our ways,
Let's try to put right what is wrong.
Pool our resources and let's take this chance
To get our lives back on song."

Taken aback by her candid approach
From this woman he'd only just met
Who wanted to alter his known way of life,
In his mind he rejected - but yet...
Perhaps, on reflection, there could be a way
To return to a life he'd once known.
Someone to care for, someone to love
In a place that could be their new home.

Four years of living a life by himself,
Four years of going downhill.
The memories of time when life was sublime,
Two years with a wife haunts him still.
A terminal illness took that away,
His decline was his only response.
How many times in the years that have passed
Did he long for what he had once.

"Perhaps it was fate that we met in that café,
Your take on a new life, I see.
Maybe it's time to make a new start,
A challenge for both you and me.
Our funds may be tight but if we use them right
This place could be made to look smart.
I'll search for a job (not done that of late!)
But it's never too late for the start!"

They both pulled together to build a new life,
Their closeness increased day-by-day.
The flat now resembled much more like a home,
Past lives were put firmly away.
The months flitted by, the plan a success,
Both enjoying their new way of life.
The next step they took was to both sign the book
And live-out their dream man and wife.

Soon they would be a family of three,
Confirmation filled both full of joy.
Their meeting by chance had led to romance
And the gift of their new baby boy.